FAIR WEATHER DAUGHTER

BY BEVERLEY H. JOHNS

ISBN: 978-1-946598-33-2

First Printing 2021

With Special Thanks to:

Carolyn Broadhead for her willingness to edit this book and two others I have written.

Marjory Lyons' Writers Group who listened to words and rewrites many times. Their contributions were greatly appreciated.

Table of Contents

Chapter One

Summer, 1955

"Mama, she tore my coloring page in half!" I cried out.

"What were you doing that you weren't supposed to do?"

"Nothing, Mama, I swear, I didn't do anything."

"Your sister wouldn't take your coloring page unless you weren't doing what you were supposed to."

I pouted, realizing it was a hopeless argument. "I didn't do anything wrong." I went in my bedroom, passing my sister with the smirk on her face. I closed my door and collapsed on my hand me down bedspread. I hated the big purple and pink flowers on it. My sister, Andrea, loved purple and pink, but she said the bedspread was worn out and she wanted a new one. Mama got her one. After all, Andrea was her perfect daughter.

Andrea was six years old when I was born. Daddy was excited to have another daughter and rocked me to sleep every night. Mama preferred to spend her time with Andrea.

I recognized my mother's favoritism to Andrea from a very young age. Andrea was always there to help Mama. She cleaned and helped her bake. Mama took Andrea everywhere with her. She was proud to show off her beautiful daughter.

When Mama's friends would ask where Patrice was, Mama would say I was pouty and jealous of my sister.

I was messy. I remember when I was three, I spilled my milk on the floor. Andrea got up and slapped me crying, "How dare you make a mess. I just cleaned the floor for Mama." She looked at Mama and said, "Mama, look what Patrice did."

At three, I expected Mama to tell Andrea she shouldn't have slapped me. Instead, Mama put her arm around Andrea as she said, "Andrea, I'm sorry. Can you help me clean it up?"

Papa looked at Mama and then said to Andrea, "You shouldn't have hit Patrice." Papa picked me up and carried me into the living room. "Come on, Patrice, let's watch TV. "

Andrea scowled at Papa. She spent the next hour cleaning the floor until Mama told her, "That's okay, Andrea, you've cleaned it up so well. The floor is spotless." Andrea beamed.

After that day, Andrea believed that Mama had given her permission to punish me when I did anything wrong. Andrea learned also that she shouldn't hit me in front of Papa.

I didn't blame Mama because she believed that Andrea was her little helper. By the time Andrea was twelve, she was cleaning the house herself. It had to be spotless. She would come home from school and clean until Papa came home and reminded her to do her homework.

Mama never seemed to bond with me. I was clumsy and not as pretty as Andrea. Every time I made a mess, she would say. "Now look at what you've done. Why can't you be neat like your sister?"

I would cry, "But. Mama, I'm trying. I'm sorry."

By the age of three, I lived in fear of my sister and faced her wrath if I spilled a cookie crumb on the floor. I knew she would hit me and then proceed to clean the floor until it was spotless.

Andrea never brought any friends to our house. I wondered whether she was afraid they might make a mess like I did.

One day, I heard Mama and Papa arguing. Papa had come home early, and Andrea was still at school. "Annie, you have to face it. There's something wrong with Andrea. All she wants to do is to clean." Mama shouted back. “Well, she’s a lot better than your Patrice. I swear she’s the messiest child alive.”

I was supposed to be taking my nap. Mother’s words cut through me. I knew Mama didn’t want me. Andrea was mean. Why couldn’t Mama see it? Just because she helped her clean all the time, she wasn’t perfect.

As the years went on, I learned how right Papa was. Andrea had serious problems. Mama denied them until it was too late.

Chapter Two

Winter of 1962

It was parent conference night at my school. I was in fourth grade, and Mama and Papa had gone to talk to my teacher. They always wanted people to think they were concerned parents.

I was sitting in front of the TV anxiously awaiting their arrival back home. I thought I was a good student, but I wasn't concerned about being tidy. Mama and my sister, Andrea, reminded me of that every day. "Teachers don't like messy students, so they won't like you." Andrea would say. I tried hard but it was difficult for me to keep all my school papers in order.

I had been left in Andrea's care that night. She came out of her bedroom periodically to snicker at me or to say, "Boy, you're going to be trouble now when Mama finds out what a poor student you are." Then she'd say, "You better enjoy that TV while you can because you won't be watching it after tonight." I had learned not to say anything because I was fearful of Andrea's wrath, especially when Papa wasn't home to protect me.

I wasn't even cognizant of what was on TV when Mama and Papa came home from the conference. I was so anxious. What if Andrea was right and I was going to fail my class?

It was a cold evening in January. Mama came in the door first, brushing snowflakes off her coat before she put it in the closet. When Andrea saw some drops on the floor from the coat, she rushed into the kitchen to get paper towels to clean up the water. Mama patted Andrea on the cheek. "Thank you, my beautiful Andrea. You are the best daughter." Mama looked over at me, her eyes cutting through me like a knife. "Patrice, I've tried so hard with you. Why can't you be like your big sister?"

I stood up from the couch but cowered and hung my head. "Mama, what did my teacher say about me? How am I doing at school?"

Andrea smirked, "I bet it was bad."

I knew Andrea was beautiful with her long dark hair and dark eyes that sparkled, sometimes with what I thought was evil. Andrea loved to clean and was so neat. I wasn't. My teacher had told me I was a good student, so I couldn't understand why Mama was upset after the conference. Had my teacher betrayed me?

Mama looked at Andrea and shook her head and frowned. She looked at me and raised her voice and shook her finger. "Do you know what your teacher said?"

I began to cry. My teacher must have said some awful things about me. "What did my teacher say?"

"You have to clean out your desk: that's what she said. Why have I been punished after all I have done for you?" Mama looked like she was going to come over and slap me but stopped as Papa came in the door.

He took off his coat and the hat that covered his bald head. "Hang up your coat and put that ugly hat away!" Mother yelled.

Papa saw the tension in the room and saw the tears in my eyes. "Why are you crying, Patrice?"

He looked at Mama. "Did you tell her the good news the teacher told us about her progress in fourth grade?"

Mama was silent.

He looked at me. "Patrice, I'm so proud of your grades, all As. That's impressive." He came over and patted me on the cheek. "That's my girl."

Chapter Three

Winter of 1962

"Patrice, I want you to behave for Andrea tonight." Mama looked up at me as we sat at the dinner table. Andrea was picking at her food. She was probably nervous about the parent conference that was about her tonight. I knew how she felt. I had been so upset about what Mama and Papa would learn about me. I was still confused about how different their perceptions were of my conference. Mama always looked for the worst in me and Papa praised the best.

I could almost feel sorry for Andrea, but when I came close to having any good feeling about her, I remembered how mean she was to me, the yelling, the slapping. In my eyes she was my beautiful, but wicked, fifteen-year-old older sister.

Papa looked over at Andrea and saw she hadn't touched her meatloaf. He saw that she didn't have any gravy on it and she usually loved meatloaf with gravy. "Here, Andrea, let me give you some gravy." He reached over and poured a little gravy on the side of her meatloaf.

Andrea stood up and pushed her plate away and yelled. "You didn't put the gravy in the center of my meatloaf. I can't eat that stuff." She cried. "It has to be in the middle." She glared at Papa, left the table, stomped to her room, yelled, "I hate you" and slammed the door.

Mama looked at Papa and scowled. "How could you upset Andrea like that?"

Papa looked confused. "Andrea loves gravy. I thought I was helping her."

"You should know that the gravy has to be in the center of the meatloaf."

My kind Father looked at Mama, shaking his head. "Not everything will always be exactly the way Andrea wants. She has to adapt." He paused, "Let's talk to the guidance counselor tonight to see if she can help."

Mama's face became scarlet. I knew that shade. It came anytime Papa questioned her actions. "What do you really know about my Andrea? Just wait til we go to her conference tonight. You'll see how perfect she is." She pointed her finger at Papa. "A counselor, really, that's the stupidest thing I have ever heard. Like she needs a counselor because all she wants is the gravy in the middle of her meatloaf. This discussion is over."

She stood up and glared at me. "Patrice, clean up the table. Papa has upset your sister. You have to clean up the table while we get ready to go to our school conference at the high school."

I nodded, "Yes, Mama, I can do it."

"It'd better be done well. And don't upset your sister any more than Papa has already."

With a sense of foreboding, I got up to clean off the table. This was not going to be a good night. I was going to be alone with my sister again. Andrea was angry and she would get even madder now that Mama was making me clean up. After all, my cleaning wouldn't live up to Andrea's standard. When Andrea saw how I had cleaned up the table and the kitchen, I would experience her wrath.

Chapter Four

Winter of 1962

I was in the kitchen cleaning up from dinner. The smell of dinner would have been pleasant any other time, but tonight it just reminded me of the scene with Andrea. I had wrapped the infamous meatloaf in aluminum foil and put it in the refrigerator. As I looked at it, I thought about what had happened at dinner and about my sister. Why did Andrea always get so upset when something wasn't cleaned well? Why did her meatloaf gravy have to be in the center of the meat? I thought about many of her quirks, like making sure that when she had a peanut butter and jelly sandwich, nothing could be showing outside the bread. Her eggs had to be cooked in bacon grease and had to be sunny side up. If the yolks broke, she wouldn't eat them.

Then I wondered whether there was something wrong with me. I didn't really care about that kind of stuff. I would rather read than clean. I loved it when Papa took me to the library. Mama never had time. She was always washing clothes or cleaning. I thought all that cleaning stuff was a waste of time. As I scrubbed the burners on the stove, I thought what was the point? The burners were just going to get dirty again in the morning when Mama cooked breakfast.

I kept scrubbing because if Andrea came out of her room and did an inspection, I would be in big trouble. I finished the cleaning as good as I could. I went into the dining room to work on my homework.

I could hear Andrea sobbing in her room. I hoped she would stay there until Mama and Papa came home from the parent conference. I learned from a very early age that when Andrea was upset, I needed to stay as far away from her as I could.

The sobbing stopped. Andrea came out of her room and headed to the bathroom. By the way she slammed the door shut, I knew she was still angry. I kept working on homework but was distracted.

When Andrea came out of the bathroom would she head back to her room, or would she come out and confront me?

It was at least fifteen minutes later when Andrea exited the bathroom, her eyes still puffy and her face in a scowl. She glared at me. "I have to get the kitchen cleaned up." She looked at the dining room table and then at me. "Who cleaned this table off?"

I looked up but didn't make eye contact. "I did it. Mama asked me to." I knew not to bring up the meatloaf scene at the dinner table.

"Hmpf, look at these crumbs. You didn't do a very good job."

I saw two small crumbs but didn't say anything. I knew not to argue with Andrea.

"Well, let me go in the kitchen and see what other mess you left."

Andrea went in the kitchen. I heard her banging pots and pans and opening cabinets.

"Oh no, what have you done?" She yelled from the kitchen.

Should I go in the kitchen or stay at the table? I pondered. It was a no-win situation no matter how you looked at it.

"Patrice, get in here right away." The decision was made for me. I knew that if I didn't follow her order she would come and get me.

I stood up and took the few steps to the kitchen. I still said nothing.

Andrea glared at me. Even with what everyone said was a beautiful face, it was very ugly in this moment. She opened one of the cabinets and took out a bowl. "Look at this." She waved the bowl at me. "This bowl does not go in this cabinet. You are so stupid."

I knew I had put the bowl in the right cabinet. Andrea must have moved it to set me up for trouble.

She continued her rant. "You are so dumb. You can't even put the bowl in the right cabinet. Papa may tell you how smart you are, but you are certainly not." Then she looked at the stove. "Look at this! You must have missed ten spots on this stove. Mama should know you can't do my job."

I realized that Andrea was angry that Mama had taken her job away from her. I remained silent. I was in trouble whatever I did.

Andrea grabbed me by my arm and shook me. "Say something, you stupid idiot." Andrea's face was that red color that signaled trouble.

I finally opened my mouth. "Andrea, please stop. You're hurting me."

Andrea let out a blood curdling laugh. "Hurting you? You haven't seen anything yet. You deserve to be hurt. You can't do anything right."

Andrea started hitting me on my arm. I tried to pull away but couldn't. She started slapping me on my face. The sting burned. I began to cry.

"Stop it right now, you big baby." She punched my arm again and then punched the other one. She then yanked me by the hair. I was scared. I didn't know what she would do next. I had to get away from her. I yanked her hands off my body and ran for my room. I locked the door and fell onto my bed. I vowed I would never be alone with my sister again. I sobbed into my pillow and whispered, "Papa, why weren't you here to protect me?

Chapter Five

Winter, 1962

I stayed locked in my room until I heard Andrea slam the door to go back in her room. I went in the bathroom and looked at my face. There were splotchy red marks in several places. My left arm hurt where she had grabbed me. I was tired. Fights with Andrea always exhausted me but this was the first time my sister had left several marks on me. I went back to my room, changed into my pajamas, and tiptoed out to the dining room to get my homework. I finished it in my room on the bed.

I didn't have a desk in my room. We only had one in the house and Mama felt it was more important for Andrea to have one since she was older and had more homework than I did. After all, I was just a fourth grader. I had locked my room again so Andrea couldn't get in. I hoped she was asleep. Sometimes I wished she was dead. I knew that thought was wrong and had never told anyone about it. After her rages, she usually went to sleep. Tonight's scene was the worst. She hadn't even been concerned that she was hurting me. I think she wanted to do so. I knew that if I hadn't gotten away from her, I would have had more bruises and maybe a broken arm or two.

The house was quiet. I had dozed off when I heard the door open. Mama was probably putting her coat in the closet. She would never throw it on the couch like I always wished I could do. When Papa came in, I knew it was him checking on me. He juggled the door. Finding it locked, he said quietly to Mama. "Looks like Patrice has locked her door again. I can't figure out why she does that."

"Just being obnoxious, no doubt. Andrea is sound asleep. She is so beautiful when she is sleeping." Mama paused. "Now that we're home, how dare you set me up like that?"

I heard Papa's response. I had climbed out of bed and was standing right by the door. "What do you mean, set you up?"

"You had those teachers call in that guidance counselor when I told you Andrea didn't need any useless person like that."

"But, Annie, you heard what the counselor said. They have to figure out what to do about Andrea. She is spending too much time on her assignments and isn't getting them done by the teachers' deadlines."

"I'll talk to her and I'm sure she'll change. She probably doesn't realize that this impacts her grades."

"How do you know she'll change, Annie?" Papa questioned Mama.

Mama continued. "I personally think it is totally unfair that the teachers are giving her D's because she doesn't turn work in. Andrea is smart. Why is it so important to complete busywork?"

I heard Papa answer. "It does matter that she isn't turning in assignments, but that guidance counselor came in, not because of the work completion, but because of that tantrum she had."

Mama was trying to keep her voice down but I could hear the anger. "Tantrum, James, really that is ridiculous. You always exaggerate everything."

I was sure glad our house was small so I could hear all of this. I wondered what my parents would think if they knew what she had done to me. I wouldn't tell them.

"Annie, face the fact. She had a tantrum and she is in high school. She slapped another girl. They could have suspended her from school."

"It was that other girl's fault."

"What do you mean? That other girl didn't do anything wrong."

"Yes, she did, she spilled some milk on Andrea's beautiful red sweater. Who wouldn't be angry about that?"

Andrea must have woken up and come out of her room. "How did my conference go, Mama?"

Mama answered, "Everything went just fine, Andrea. I'm so proud of you. Go back to bed."

Chapter Six

Winter, 1962

Our family had our usual morning ritual. We all ate together, and Mama made eggs and bacon. Since Andrea's eggs had to be sunny side up, if Mama made a mistake and broke them, Papa and I got those. Getting ready this morning, I had seen the number of bruises on my arms and was glad it was winter. I could cover them up with my long-sleeved yellow sweater that had been handed down to me from my sister. Even though my clothes were old, they were still nice because Mama bought beautiful things for Andrea. I couldn't cover up the welts on my face but hoped no one noticed.

As I sat down at the table, Andrea was already there, sipping on her orange juice and frowning.

"What's the matter with your orange juice, Andrea?" Mama asked.

"It has too much pulp in it. Yuk, I can't drink this."

Mama picked up the juice glass. "Oh, my goodness, you're right. Let me strain it for you."

"Thank you, Mama." She smiled. After Mama left the room, Andrea glared at me. I knew what she meant by that look. Keep your mouth shut.

Papa had his nose in the newspaper and looked up at me. "Patrice, what are those marks on your face?"

I put my head down as I answered. I hated lying to him but knew I had to. "There were some bugs in my room last night. They were biting my face."

"Probably because your room is so dirty." Andrea said.

"Oh, my goodness. Remind me, I'll check your room when I get off work today." After Papa worked hard all day at the factory, I hated for him to have to come home and try to spray my room for bugs. I knew though I had no choice but to continue this lie.

"Thanks, Papa." I smiled. I wished that Papa could realize that my sister did this.

Andrea looked at me and smiled. I had given Papa the right answer.

When I boarded the school bus in the front of the house, some of the kids asked me what the marks were on my face. "Did you get in a fight?" "What's wrong with your face?" I gave the same answer I gave Papa.

Why was everyone looking at my face anyway? Mama had told me it was a plain one, not beautiful like

Andrea's. I didn't think I was ugly. My nose was a little big for my face, but people told me I had pretty brown eyes and golden blond hair, just like Papa. I was glad I didn't look like my sister. Her jet-black hair and dark eyes only masked her evil personality.

When I got to my fourth-grade classroom, my teacher greeted all of us as we came in the door. I loved seeing her. "Good morning," she said. I put my head down so she couldn't see my face.

Chapter Seven

Winter, 1962

I hoped my teacher wouldn't focus any attention on me today. I tried not to look at her. I even put my head down on my desk a few times. When it was time for restroom break, I walked by my teacher, Mrs. Corey. In almost a whisper she asked me to see her. What was I going to do? I couldn't look at her. She asked the teacher across the hall to watch the rest of my class and told me to come with her. I did what I was told. That hallway seemed so long and dark today. My hands were shaking. What would I say?

We went into the principal's office. I started crying. I was in trouble and hadn't done anything wrong. Had Mama called the school and told them I was bad last night?

Mrs. Corey led me into Mr. Dennison's office and closed the door. I was sobbing. Mr. Dennison was a big man with a bald head and a fat belly. I had never had to go to his office before.

My teacher put her arm around me. I grimaced because there was a sharp pain in my arm. I sobbed even more. Mrs. Corey pulled away, brushed my hair away from my face and asked me to tell her what happened.

Between sobs, I answered, "I, I got bit by some bugs."

My teacher responded, "I'm sorry. Your face must really hurt from those bug bites." She paused. "Does your arm hurt?"

I looked down, "I guess I slept on it wrong."

"Can I look at it?" This big man said in a low voice.

I couldn't tell the principal no, so I nodded my head and said, "Okay."

My teacher asked me to take my sweater off.

I did what I was told. I saw the frown on Mrs. Corey and Mr. Dennison's face. They didn't look happy.

I put my head down. "I'm sorry."

Mrs. Corey rubbed my back, "Patrice, you're not in trouble. Can you tell me what happened?"

I nodded my head and a wave of salty tears streamed down my face. "I was bad."

"What did you do? You can tell us." Mr. Dennison asked.

"I didn't clean up the kitchen right."

Mrs. Corey continued to keep her arm on my back. That made me feel better. "Did your mother hit you because you didn't clean the kitchen right?"

Through my sobs, I shook my head no. Mr. Dennison looked at my teacher and said, "Let me go check on your class and you stay here with Patrice."

"Did your father hit you?" Mr. Dennison quizzed.

"No." I looked up at my teacher.

"Who did this to you then?" Mrs. Corey looked down at me. "Let's sit down until you feel better." She motioned for me to sit in one of the two chairs in Mr. Dennison's office.

I was glad he left. I felt better knowing that he wasn't going to punish me for the marks my sister had made.

Mrs. Corey and I sat in silence for a few minutes. I felt safe with her, but she couldn't protect me from my sister. She got up from her chair and came over and knelt in front of me. "Patrice, I have to tell some people so this can't happen again. If someone hurt you, I want to make sure you are okay." She paused. "Do you understand I want to help you?"

I looked at Mrs. Corey and felt the warmth and caring she had for me. When I grew up, I wanted to be just like her. She was beautiful with her blond hair, and she always smelled like a flower. I didn't know what to do. I didn't want to get Mama and Papa in trouble. They didn't know.

Mrs. Corey asked, "Are you sure your mother and father didn't do it?"

I blurted out. "It wasn't Mama or Papa. It was my sister, Andrea."

Chapter Eight

Winter, 1962

Why did I tell Mrs. Corey? What was going to happen to me? Andrea was going to be real mad. Couldn't anyone protect me from her? I rode the bus home from school. I was always home before Andrea. I opened the door and heard Mama yell from the kitchen, "Patrice, get to your room and start your homework." Had Mama already found out?

I was thirsty. "Can I have a glass of water, Mama?"

"Get in here and get the water out of the faucet. Quit trying to stall from doing your homework."

I went in the kitchen, got a glass and ran the faucet for my water.

"Wash your face. Those bug bites on your face still look bad and your eyes are swollen. Maybe hot water will help."

"Yes, Mama." I thought that no amount of hot water was going to make the marks made by Andrea go away. I wished Andrea would disappear.

Dinnertime was quiet with little conversation. I was hoping we wouldn't have another scene between Papa and Andrea. We had a SPAM casserole tonight. Even though it was my favorite meal, I didn't have much of an appetite. Papa asked how my day went at school. I just said, "Okay." Papa looked at Andrea. "Andrea, how was your day?"

"Everyone thought my new sweater that Mama got me was beautiful." She smiled at her mother. "Thank you, Mama."

"Only the best for my sweetheart," Mama answered as she poured Andrea some more milk.

I thought school should be about what you learned, but what was important to Andrea and Mama was what you wore.

As Andrea helped Mama clean up the table, there was a knock on the door. Papa said. "I'll get it." As he opened the door, there was a mean looking skinny lady wearing a black suit. She had her hair pulled up in a bun. "Good evening," she said, "Are you Mr. Porter?"

"Yes, that's right. Can I help you? We just finished dinner so don't want to buy anything this week."

"I need to come in and talk with you and your wife." She showed a card that I thought must have been an identification badge. "I'm from Child Protective Services."

Father had a very confused look on his face. He stammered. “You must have the wrong home.”

“Mr. Porter, this is the right house.” She took another two steps into the living room.

“Okay, what’s this about?” Papa asked. I had backed away from the door and was moving toward my room.

She pointed at me, “Is this Patrice?”

“Yes” Papa answered. “What’s the matter?”

The mean skinny lady looked at me and then answered Papa. “I need to see her and talk with her.” She paused. “Is your wife here?”

Papa called for Mama, “Annie, can you come in here?”

Mama came in the living room from the kitchen as she was wringing her hands with the tea towel. “What’s going on?”

The lady spoke up, “I’m here to see Patrice and talk with both of you.” She moved her glasses further up on her face. “Is your other daughter here?”

“Yes, of course, Andrea is here. She’s cleaning up the kitchen.” Mama looked at me. “What does this have to do with Andrea? Has Patrice done something wrong?”

"No, Mrs. Porter, Patrice has done nothing wrong." The lady frowned at Mama.

Andrea came out of the kitchen and saw the strange lady in the living room. "What's going on? Is she selling something?"

"Are you Andrea?" The woman asked. Andrea looked at Mama as if to say do I have to do what this mean woman says?

Mama smiled at her older daughter, "Yes, we need you to go to your room. Don't worry about anything."

The lady looked at me, "Patrice, can I talk to you with your Mother and Father? Can you sit down on the couch?" I sat down on our blue and green flowered couch. The lady sat down next to me. She looked at my swollen face. I started crying. Mama scowled at me from her chair in the living room. "Patrice, you need to tell this lady what you've done."

The lady glared at Mama, "Mrs. Porter, your daughter hasn't done anything wrong. We have reason to believe somebody in this house has hurt her."

"That's ridiculous." Mama stood up. "You need to leave right now."

Papa was in his easy chair, "Sit down, Annie. We need to listen to what this lady says."

Mama listened to Papa. I was surprised she sat down.

"Patrice, that's a pretty sweater you have on, but I need you to take it off for me." The lady directed me.

I looked at Papa and saw him nodding for me to do what I was asked to do. I took my sweater off slowly and very carefully because my arms still hurt from Andrea's tantrum. I hoped I didn't have to take my blouse off in front of this strange lady.

Papa gasped when he saw my arms. "What happened, Patrice?" I put my head down. Mama asked. "Were you climbing again on the school playground?" I shook my head no.

The skinny lady looked at me. She had me hold my arms out. The bruises had gotten darker since last night. I started crying. "I'm so sorry, I won't do it again."

"Do what again?" The lady said in almost a whisper. "You didn't do anything wrong."

I sobbed, "I didn't clean the kitchen very good."

"You never do," Mama said. "What's that got to do with your arms being bruised?"

The woman stared at Mama and then looked at me. "Patrice, thank you. You can go to your room now so I can talk to your mother and father."

I got up and just stood there. Papa got up. "Patrice, come give me a hug. It'll be okay. See you in the morning."

I gave Papa a light hug. His arms were there to protect me. Mama frowned, "Get in your room and get your homework done."

Chapter Nine

Winter 1962

I closed my door and was thankful I had gotten all my homework done before supper. I sat on the floor close to my door. I was glad our house had paper thin walls so I could hear the conversations among the skinny lady, Mama, and Papa. Was this lady going to take me away from my home?

The skinny lady who had identified herself from Child Protective Services said in a low voice, "Mr. and Mrs. Porter, this is serious. We have reason to believe that your daughter Andrea put those bruises on Patrice." She paused. "I need to talk with her. Can you ask her to come out of her room?"

Mama raised her voice. "I told you before. This is ridiculous. Our beautiful Andrea would never hurt anyone. Patrice was probably climbing on the playground and got those bruises on her arm."

Papa spoke, "Annie, go get Andrea out of her room."

"I will not." Mama yelled. "Get out of this house right now. Who do you think you are barging in here?"

I heard the lady from Child Protective Services raise her voice. “Mrs. Porter. I am from Child Protective Services. My job is to protect your daughter, Patrice, who has been hurt in this very house. It is not to your benefit to protect your other daughter.”

Papa said in his very soft voice, “Annie, do what the lady has asked.”

“I will not, whose side are you on anyway?”

The lady from Child Protective Services answered, “This isn’t about sides. Mrs. Porter, if you choose not to cooperate, I have no choice but to take Patrice with me and place her in a safe place.”

I was sweating and shaking. Was this lady going to take me away? Could Papa stop her? I was scared that Mama wouldn’t care if I was taken away. After all, Mama didn’t seem to care about me. Andrea was more important. Tears streamed from my eyes, and I wanted to sob aloud, but I knew I had to be silent.

“Oh, very well, I’ll get my Andrea, but you’ll see how wonderful she is. You’ll find out that she would never hurt anyone. We’re a loving family.” Mama paused. “There are plenty of other families whose children should be taken away from them.” Mama stammered. “Why don’t you spend your time taking their children away?”

Mama must have moved toward Andrea’s door. “Andrea, can you come out here sweetie?”

I heard Andrea say, "What's she still doing here?" "What is this about?"

Papa answered, "Andrea, come sit down; this lady needs to talk to you."

The lady answered her, "Andrea, can you tell me what happened last night?"

"What do you mean? Mama and Papa went to a conference at the high school last night to find out how well I'm doing. I'm a freshman this year."

"Did you stay with your sister?"

"Yes, I had to take care of her. It was hard. She always misbehaves."

"Did she misbehave last night?" I heard the lady ask.

I wanted to stand up, open my door, and shout that I didn't misbehave.

"Oh yes," Andrea answered. "She does every time I take care of her. Mama knows, tell them."

Mama said, "Just tell the lady what Patrice did."

Andrea answered, "She didn't clean up all the crumbs and put the dishes away wrong."

The lady answered, "Did that make you mad, Andrea?"

"Well, of course, she knows how to clean up." Andrea paused. "I usually do all the cleaning, but I was upset with Papa last night because he ruined my meatloaf."

Mama joined in the conversation. "Andrea is a wonderful little housekeeper. I just don't know what I'd do without her."

I got up off my floor and got my teddy bear and hugged it tight. If this lady took me away, would I be able to take my bear with me? Where would I go? Would I be able to go to school? I sat back down on the floor.

The lady asked another question, "Andrea, did you punish your sister when she misbehaved?"

"Oh yes, I had to. Mama would have been so upset if she would have come back home and found the mess Patrice left."

I wanted to shout that I never left a mess. I was tired of Andrea needing to have everything spotless.

The lady asked, "Did you hit your sister?"

Andrea answered, "Just a couple of times to make her behave. That's okay. Mama always told me to do what I needed to make Patrice do what I wanted her to do."

Mama spoke up, "Andrea, sweetie, did you hit her on the face?"

"Only once, Mama, then I just hit her arm." Andrea paused. "Why's this lady asking all these questions? I was just making Patrice clean."

The lady answered, "Andrea, you can go back to your room."

I heard Andrea close her door.

The lady waited a minute. I was sweating more even though it was the dead of winter. Was she going to come in and take me away? I locked my door. "Mr. and Mrs. Porter, Andrea abused Patrice and my report is going to show this report as founded. Since this is the first time this has happened, I'm not going to take Patrice away from you."

"That would be absurd. Andrea was just making her mind." Mama said.

Papa spoke up, "Andrea can't be hitting her sister. I assure you we won't let this happen again."

"I'm glad to hear that, Mr. Porter. However, your daughter needs professional help."

Mama raised her voice again, "She needs no such thing. She doesn't have any problems."

"Mrs. Porter, I will be sending you and your husband an official letter that says that Patrice can never be left alone with Andrea again."

I was glad to hear that. The lady wasn't going to take me away. I hugged my bear.

The lady continued, "The letter also is going to order both of you to take your daughter to counseling sessions at least five times."

Mama got louder. "We are not going to counseling. There is nothing wrong with our daughter Andrea. Patrice needs to behave."

I heard the lady say, "Mr. and Mrs. Porter, if you do not comply, both of your daughters will be taken away from you."

Chapter Ten

Spring, 1964

Andrea was a junior in high school, getting ready for her high school prom. It had been two years since that eventful night when I thought I was going to be taken away from Mama and Papa. I wouldn't have missed Andrea or Mama, but what would I have done without my Papa. Mama and Andrea hated me. I felt it every time they looked at me. They blamed me for what happened. Mama and Papa did what they were told by Child Protective Services. They never left me alone with Andrea again. When they went to the ordered counseling sessions, they got a babysitter. They never went anywhere else together unless they took me with them.

Those counseling sessions didn't seem to do anything to improve Andrea and Mama's meanness. They never hit me, but they hurt me with their words. They called me dumb and ugly. I would have believed them, but Papa told me I was smart and pretty. My grades at school were always "A's" so I couldn't be too dumb. I would never forget how Mrs. Corey, my fourth-grade teacher, helped me. She did care about me and even in fifth and sixth grade checked up on me.

One day when I was in sixth grade, Mrs. Corey stopped me in the hall, “Patrice, I just got the forms for a writing contest. I think you should enter since you are such a good writer. Will you write something, and I’ll help you send it in?”

I read the directions and wrote an essay about Papa, my hero. Mrs. Corey helped me fill out the application. I won the contest sponsored by the local Kiwanis Club. They had a banquet. I was invited so I could be awarded a certificate. Mrs. Corey said she would be there. I went home to tell Mama and Papa and asked them to go with me. Papa was excited, “Patrice, I wouldn’t miss it.”

I didn’t tell Papa it was about him. I wanted him to be surprised.

On the day of the banquet, I got up excited to go to school. My class had a party for me. They had white cake with lots of icing, my favorite. My sixth-grade teacher said she would be there, as would Mrs. Corey. I felt so good that day. Mama and Papa would go to the banquet. Papa would be surprised about what I had written.

I got home from school and went to my room and started getting ready. I wanted to wear my best dress even if it was a hand-me-down from my sister. It was a pretty pink dress with flowers on the hem.

Papa came home early that day. I think he was as excited as I was. I went out in the living room. Andrea must have been in her room. Papa had dressed up in his Sunday suit and Mama had her beige dress that she wore to church sometimes.

"Well, Patrice, you look as pretty as a picture. I'm so proud of you." Papa smiled. "I'll go get the car out."

"Let me say bye to Andrea." Mama said.

Papa frowned, "I thought she was going with us?"

"No, she said she wants to have her friend, Janis, over to talk about the prom. You know how important prom is."

"Well okay, but I was hoping we could all go as a family." Papa put his head down.

Andrea came out of her room and sniffled and coughed. "Oh mama, I don't feel good."

"What's the matter, sweetheart?"

"I'm so sick, Mama, will you stay home with me?"

"Of course, Andrea. I don't need to go to any silly banquet. You're more important to me."

Chapter Eleven

Spring, 1964

Papa and I went to the banquet by ourselves that night. I will never forget the look on his face when they read my essay and asked me to come forward to accept my certificate. I saw a few tears run down his face as they read my tribute to my Papa, my hero.

Andrea was feeling fine when we got home. I realized she had faked her illness to keep Mama from going. We never told Mama that the essay was about Papa.

My essay later won the state award. My teachers and Papa all drove two hours to see me recognized. Mama said she was too busy getting ready for Andrea's prom.

I heard her tell Papa one night, "It's so silly that they're making such a big deal about a story Patrice wrote." She laughed and continued, "Like that's such an accomplishment. She sure could never make a living as a writer."

Papa answered her, "Now you listen to me, Annie. Patrice is a very smart and talented girl. It's about time you were proud of her."

Mama responded, “Humpf. Proud of her for writing some stupid essay. It’s more important for us to spend our time on Andrea’s prom and getting her ready to graduate next year.”

“What do you mean getting ready for her graduation? If she doesn’t finish the work she has to do right now, she’s not going to get a diploma next year.”

“Of course, she will get her diploma. She only has three term papers to get done this semester. “I’m helping her with those.”

“Helping her or writing them for her, Annie? How many more papers are you going to do for her?”

Chapter Twelve

Spring, 1964

Andrea was chosen for the Prom Court. One of the female members would be queen. Andrea and Mama had picked out a beautiful dress for the prom before they knew that Andrea was on the court. One night after dinner when we were all sitting in the living room, Mama showed the dress to Papa. The price tag was still on it. Papa looked at the dress and then at the tag, "Annie, this is way too much money."

"Oh James, Andrea has to have a beautiful dress to accentuate how pretty she is. Besides, we'll keep the dress and when and if Patrice goes to her prom, that is if anyone asks her and she isn't too fat for the dress, she'll be able to wear it." Mama laughed. "Two for one."

The announcement about Andrea being on the court was made a week before the prom. The day after, Andrea came in the door from school, slamming the wood behind her. "Mama, where are you?"

I came out of my room and saw the tears in her eyes. "Andrea, what's wrong?"

Andrea sobbed, "Oh go back in your room, you ugly thing."

Mama came out and saw the tears in Andrea's eyes. "What's wrong, sweetheart?"

Andrea sniffled, "I can't wear the dress I have."

"Why not?" Mama frowned.

"It's lavender."

I was standing close to my door but hadn't gone back in my room. I didn't have to do everything Andrea told me. "But that's your favorite color."

Andrea scowled at me, "Stupid, Sissy Moore is wearing a lavender dress."

"Oh no" Mama said. "Can't you wear the same color as Sissy?"

"No, I hate her. I would never wear the same color dress as that bitch."

Mama scowled, "Andrea, watch your language around your sister."

Through her tears, Andrea laughed, "Like she's never used that word." She stopped and took a breath, "Mama, I have to get another dress."

Without thinking that I would incur more of my sister's wrath, I said, "Papa said your lavender dress was too expensive. You can't buy another one."

She gave me a dirty look, "Well, we'll just see about that." She went in her room and slammed the door.

"Andrea, it's time for dinner." Mama called her to the table about an hour later. I was already seated and we were having tuna casserole tonight. Papa asked me about my school day.

"I got an A on my math test." I bragged. "I was the only one who got an A in my whole class."

Andrea heard my comment as she sat down at the dinner table. "Who cares about your math test?" She paused. "Papa, I have to get a different dress for the prom."

"What's wrong with the one you have?" Papa asked.

"It's lavender and Sissy Moore on the prom court is wearing the same color."

Papa smiled, "That's okay. Two girls can wear the same color."

"No, I can't. I hate her and don't want to wear the same color she has."

"Well then," Papa took a scoop of the tuna casserole and passed it to me. "Take the dress you got back and get a new one."

"But I don't want to take that dress back. I like it. I want to keep it."

"You can't have both, Andrea. I have to work hard to pay for one dress. You are not getting two dresses."

Andrea stood up from the table and cried as she pointed at me. "You'd get her two dresses if she wanted them but, oh no, you can't spend the money for me." Andrea stared at me and went to her room and slammed the door.

"James, did you have to upset Andrea?" Mama asked. "It's a big honor for her to be on the prom court. This is a once in a lifetime experience for her. We can't ruin it. I'll go talk to her."

Papa said in his firm voice, "Just take the lavender dress back and get another one, preferably a cheaper one."

Mama went to Andrea's room. Papa and I kept eating the tuna casserole. We didn't say anything. I hoped that Andrea would just agree to take the lavender dress back.

About five minutes later, Andrea and Mama came out of Andrea's room. Andrea carried the dress on the hanger. "Papa, I can't take this dress back."

"Why not?" Papa asked. "Annie, don't you have the receipt?"

Andrea pointed to a spot on the bottom of the dress's hem, "Look at this. The dress has a bad spot on it. I saw Patrice looking at my dress the other day. She must have spilled something on it."

Chapter Thirteen

Spring, 1964

Andrea got her new dress. She lied about me spilling something on it. I had never even been near her stupid dress.

Prom night came. Mama was busy fixing Andrea's beautiful dark hair. She had put it up in a French twist. The new dress Andrea got was a pink one with lots of sequins on it. It fit Andrea tight in the waist and then puffed out into a full skirt. It did look nice on her, I had to admit. I went to my room once Andrea was dressed. I figured that she didn't want to introduce me to her date for the night. Billy Schroder was his name. Andrea had never been out with him before. She always had lots of dates, but she never had the same one more than twice. I never asked her why but always wondered whether none of them were perfect enough for her.

The doorbell rang. Papa went to answer it while I stayed in my room, and Mama continued to help Andrea get ready.

"Good evening, Mr. Porter. Is Andrea ready?"

"Come in, young man." Papa answered. "I'm sure Andrea will be ready in a few minutes." Papa paused. "Patrice come out and say hello to Billy."

I crept out of my room. I knew Andrea wouldn't be happy if she saw me talking to Billy. She wouldn't want him to know she had an ugly sister.

"Billy, this is Patrice, Andrea's sister." Papa said.

"Pleased to meet you, Patrice. I didn't know Andrea had a sister. Where do you go to school?"

"I'm in sixth grade at Adams School."

"Uh your sister is beautiful." As an afterthought, he added. "Oh, you are too."

"Thank you." I hung my head down embarrassed. I knew he was just saying that to be kind.

I looked Billy over. He was wearing a white tuxedo with a light blue shirt. His blond hair was slicked down. He did look handsome. I found myself dreaming of what it would be like to date a guy so nice looking when I went to a prom.

Andrea made her entrance into the living room. She frowned at me when she saw me and then put a smile on her face when she saw Billy. I knew that smile she used when she was trying to manipulate someone.

Billy stood up. "Oh Andrea, you look so beautiful." He stared at her and then said. "I brought you a corsage."

I looked at the corsage. It was pink to match her dress, but it had two purple flowers in it. I knew Andrea wouldn't like that because the purple would remind her of Sissy Moore's dress.

Andrea looked at the corsage and then at Mama. Mama said, "The pink flowers are so pretty, but it might look better if I take the two purple flowers out. Is that okay?"

Billy had a puzzled look on his face. "Sure, Mrs. Porter, whatever you say, if it's okay with Andrea."

Mama took the corsage out to the kitchen. In a few minutes she brought it back without the purple flowers. "Here this looks better. Let Billy pin it on your dress and I'll take a picture of the two of you."

Billy and Andrea left for the prom. I wondered whether Andrea would become queen and Billy would be king. I had heard Andrea tell Mama that the king and queen were voted on separately, and if Andrea became queen, which she was convinced she would, Billy might not be king. It might be one of the other boys. I thought that Andrea didn't care about Billy. She was just concerned that she would be queen.

I went to bed that night hoping that Andrea would be queen, not because I thought she deserved it but because I knew Andrea would be hard to live with if she didn't get it. She always talked about how she someday would be prom queen.

I awakened in the middle of the night when the door slammed shut. I knew that Andrea had not been crowned the queen.

Chapter Fourteen

Spring, 1965

Andrea had sulked about not becoming prom queen when she was a junior. She had gotten mad at Billy, her date, for being prom king, and I heard her tell Mama she would never forgive him for accepting Prom King without her being the Queen. That was the end of their relationship.

From the conversations, I heard Mama and Papa have, Andrea might not graduate. She wasn't turning in assignments. I couldn't imagine that. I wouldn't dream of not doing my assignments and turned them in early any chance I got. Andrea just didn't seem to care about school.

One night at dinner, Papa asked Andrea whether she had completed all her work.

Andrea replied, "Don't worry, Papa, I got an A on my last paper. Mama helped me."

"How many more do you need to get done?" Papa asked.

"Only three more."

"But it's only three weeks until graduation and you have senior prom next weekend," Papa commented.

Mama spoke up, "I'll get them typed for her, James; don't worry."

"Thanks, Mama." Andrea answered. "And prom this year is no big deal. I'm not even going."

"What?" Papa opened his mouth.

"I just met Jesse this week and he thinks proms are stupid."

"Who is this young man? We haven't met him yet."

"No, Papa, he goes to the private high school, Saint Ambrose. I met him at the Big Boy after school when I was there with my friend, Janis."

"Is he graduating this year, sweetie?" Mama asked.

"Yes, and he's going away to college in Connecticut." Andrea paused. "Mama, you should see the red Mustang he drives."

I was impressed about the Mustang he drove. I loved those cars, but knew it was better not to say anything that Andrea could argue with.

"When are we going to meet this Jesse?" Papa asked.

"Oh, I don't know." Andrea stammered. "One of these days. He lives over in the Lincoln Park subdivision; you know where the rich people live."

Papa looked at me as I was finishing up my dessert. "Patrice, will you go to your room so Mama and I can talk to Andrea?"

I understood that cue. Papa was going to try to find out what Andrea was up to. "Sure, Papa."

I went to my room and started working on my homework. I heard Papa say. "Andrea, what's going on between you and this young man, Jesse?"

"Papa, he's a nice boy. He took me for a drive in his Mustang and said he'll take me out that night, not to some childish prom."

"Oh good, I'll get to meet him then." Papa answered.

I heard Andrea raise her voice. "I'm not having him pick me up here. He's rich. Our house is so beneath him."

Chapter Fifteen

Spring, 1965

Andrea would be graduating from high school in two weeks. Mama and Papa argued that Mama had written Andrea's senior project for her. One night after I had gone to bed, I heard them talking. "Annie, you can't keep covering for Andrea. She should be doing her own assignments."

"Oh, James, who cares about those papers? They're just busy work anyway. The important thing is that Andrea graduate."

"But what's she going to do after graduation? She hasn't even started looking for a job," Papa commented.

"I think Andrea's in love with that nice young man."

"She barely knows him, and we've never met him."

Mama raised her voice. "We know he's going to college out east and he's rich and has a nice car. What else is there we need to know?"

"Annie, we really don't know who he is. We should meet his parents."

"James, you worry too much. Andrea is pretty and will make this young man a good wife."

Papa got loud. “Wife? She just met this guy. Annie, we know our Andrea has problems, and she is going to have trouble in relationships.”

“Humph, we’ll just see about that. I know our darling daughter will marry her prince and live happily ever after.”

“Don’t count on that. Life isn’t a fairy tale.”

I heard the door close. Andrea must have come in the house from her date with Jesse.

Mama commented, “Hi, honey, how was your date?”

“Hi Mama, what are you and Papa doing still up? I thought you’d be asleep.”

Papa answered. “We were waiting up for you. It’s eleven-thirty on a school night. You know you’re supposed to be in at eleven.”

“Oh, Papa, I’m graduating in two weeks anyway, so it doesn’t matter what time I come in. I’m grown up now.”

I could just picture Andrea’s manipulative and controlling smile.

Papa raised his voice. “Young lady, when you live under this roof that you don’t seem to think is good enough for you, you’ll follow my rules.”

"James don't be so hard on Andrea. She is almost out of school and will be looking for a job soon."

Andrea laughed and raised her voice. "A job? I'm not going to need a job."

I heard Papa ask, "Just what is that supposed to mean, young lady?"

"Jesse has asked me to marry him, and I said yes."

Chapter Sixteen

Spring, 1965

What should have been a day for celebration started with a hateful moment that stuck with me for the rest of my life. Andrea's graduation day was a swirl of activities. Mama had planned a graduation party for her. We had very little extended family. Mama's parents had died before I was born. We never talked about what had happened to them, but I had never known a grandma or grandpa. When I asked Mama about them, she just said they went to heaven. She didn't want to talk about them. Mama had a sister, Aunt Betty. Aunt Betty and Uncle George never came around much but were coming for the graduation party after the ceremony.

Papa had always called himself an orphan. He never knew his parents and was raised in the Soldier's and Sailor's Children's home. He had no family to invite to his daughter's high school graduation. He had a friend there at the home. Papa always called Harold his best friend. Papa would go over to Harold's house a couple of times a week. Mama hated Harold and told Papa that she should be his best friend. I suspected Papa went over there to get away from Mama. Harold and his wife were coming to the party.

A few of our neighbors had been invited, not because of Mother or Andrea, but because Papa was always doing things to help others out. He mowed the grass for a month when one of the neighbors was in the hospital. He shoveled snow for the ladies who had lost their husbands and were elderly. Papa was always kind to others. Mama, on the other hand, didn't invite the neighbors into the house because she feared they would track in some dirt.

Jesse and his parents had been invited to the party, but we didn't know whether they were coming or not. Andrea had made it clear that our home was embarrassing to her and she didn't know whether they would want to come.

At breakfast that morning, Andrea had gotten into an argument with Papa. While we were eating our bacon and eggs, Papa asked, "Are we going to get to meet Jesse and his parents tonight at your party?"

Andrea took a sip of her orange juice and answered, "I don't know, Papa. They aren't used to coming to this side of town."

"And just what side of town is this, Andrea?" Papa asked.

"You know, Papa."

"No, I don't. Why don't you explain it to me?"

Andrea put her juice glass down. “Face it Papa, we live on the wrong side of town. We don’t live in the rich area, like Jesse does.”

Papa’s face was getting red. “Young lady, let me explain to you that our home is just fine. You have a wonderful roof over your head, plenty to eat, and you get all the clothes you want.”

“Mama knows what I mean. This house isn’t very big and the furniture is at least as old as I am, isn’t that right?” Andrea looked to Mama for her support.

“James, you know what Andrea means. We do have to watch our money, and I haven’t had a new couch for years.”

I spoke up, “I like our house and the couch.”

Andrea scowled at me. When she stood up, I thought she was going to hit me. Instead, she picked up her plate, glass, and silverware, and took them to the kitchen. When she came back in the dining room, she stood by the table. “I certainly would be so embarrassed for Jesse and his parents to meet you anyway.”

Papa stood up. “Andrea, go to your room and think about this. If we don’t meet your standards for living, then I am sure we don’t meet your standards for paying for a wedding.” He paused and pointed his finger in her face. This was the first time I had ever seen Papa do this. “If Jesse and his parents are too good to come to our home for your graduation party, then I am too good to pay for any wedding. You can elope for all I care."

Andrea screamed. "I hate you. You never want to do anything for me, just your precious Patrice." She pointed to me and screamed. "And you never wanted her in the first place."

Mama and I both stood up. Mama said, "Andrea, that is quite enough. We don't need to talk about that now."

"Why not?" Andrea yelled. "You know you didn't want her; you wanted a boy."

I was confused as I looked from one of my parents to the other, "What do you mean, you didn't want me, Mama, Papa? That can't be."

Andrea got up in my face and yelled, "Why do you think you are called Patrice? Mama and Papa thought they were having a boy." She laughed, "You were supposed to be Patrick. Nobody wanted you."

Chapter Seventeen

Graduation Night, 1965

Andrea's graduation ceremony and the party were a blur for me until the end of the evening. I still felt like a piece of my heart had been stolen from me. How could Mama and Papa not want me? I was shocked that they wanted me to be Patrick. That explained Mama's aloofness from me but what about Papa? He had talked to me after Andrea slapped her hurtful comment in my face. He said that he was happy to have me as his daughter and was happy when he found out I was a girl. Mama said nothing, so I knew she had wanted Patrick, not me.

Jesse had driven Andrea from graduation to our house for the party. Once he got there, he called his parents to ask them to come over. Papa's friend, Harold and his wife were there as were a few neighbors.

Aunt Betty and Uncle George came in right after Andrea had arrived. When Andrea saw them, she looked at them and said, "Oh, I didn't know you were coming. You always seem so busy doing other things." Aunt Betty ignored Andrea and came over to me, gave me a big hug, and said, "Oh Patrice, it's so good to see you. Now that school is out you can spend some time over at our house." Aunt Betty and Uncle George didn't have children and were always inviting Andrea and me over, but Mama never would allow us to go. I liked them and would have enjoyed visiting them. They seemed so kind to me.

Mama had set a beautiful table. She put her best crocheted tablecloth on our dining room table, had a big punchbowl full of Hawaiian Punch, and had a dish of nuts and of mints on the table. The cake had beautiful purple and pink roses on it with the inscription, "Congratulations, Andrea."

Andrea hugged and kissed Jesse on the cheek. She was ignoring everyone else. I heard the doorbell ring and said, "I'll get it." Andrea put her hand out to stop me, "I'll get it, it's probably Jesse's parents."

Andrea was right. It was Jesse's mother and father. Andrea opened the door with a big grin plastered on her face. "Good evening, Mr. and Mrs. Payton, come in. I'm so glad you would take time out of your schedule to come here for a little while." Andrea focused on them until Papa said, "Andrea, will you introduce your guests to everyone here."

I detected Andrea's look of disapproval mixed with her phony smile, "Everybody, this is Mr. and Mrs. Payton, my fiancé Jesse's parents.

Mr. Payton did a wave at the people here as he took over, "Hi, everyone, thank you for inviting us to our future daughter-in-law's graduation ceremony. We are so happy to welcome Andrea into our family and know that

Andrea and Jesse will have a wonderful life to come." He paused. "Andrea, Jesse's mother and I want to present you with this gift for your future." He pulled an envelope out of his pocket.

Andrea put her hands to her face acting like she was in shock. "Oh, Mr. Payton, what is this? You didn't have to give me anything." She looked at the envelope as she asked, "Can I open it?"

"You sure can." Mrs. Payton answered. "It's our way of saying we are delighted to have you in our family and want to help out with the costs of the wedding."

Andrea was beaming. She opened the envelope and gasped. "Oh my goodness, it's such a generous gift. Mama, look, this is a check for $2,000." She giggled and hugged Mrs. Payton. "Now I can buy that beautiful wedding dress I told you I wanted, but Papa couldn't afford."

Chapter Eighteen

Graduation night, 1965

Papa's face turned red when Andrea responded that he couldn't afford the wedding dress that Andrea wanted. With relatives and neighbors there, he contained his anger and calmly said to Mr. and Mrs. Payton, "That is very generous of you. Maybe you and Jesse can stay after the party this evening and we can discuss it further." Papa looked like he could explode, but I admired his composure. I guessed what choice did he have. Andrea, once again, had manipulated the situation to get what she wanted.

"Of course, we can stay after. We just haven't had a chance to get to know your beautiful family well," Mrs. Payton responded.

To change the subject, Mama asked Andrea to cut her cake. I wondered whether she had been part of Andrea's scheme to get an expensive wedding dress. "Dear, how about if you cut your beautiful cake for everyone? I'm sure everyone wants a piece of it to celebrate graduation and your engagement."

Several people spoke through the tension filled room, "Here, here, Andrea, cut your cake."

"Jesse do help me cut it. After all, we're partners now." Andrea smiled and kissed Jesse on the lips. I thought that Jesse probably was very infatuated with Andrea because he didn't really know her. On the other hand, I realized more every day that Andrea saw him as her ticket to wealth.

It was at that point that I had an epiphany that Andrea would soon leave our home, and I wouldn't have to put up with her conniving anymore on a daily basis. I knew she would always be my sister and would be a source of angst for me, but at least I wouldn't need to see her so much of the time.

Soon after the cake was served, the guests began to leave. The atmosphere of celebration was gone after Andrea's announcement about her wedding dress.

As Aunt Betty and Uncle George prepared to leave, Uncle George asked Papa if he could see him in the kitchen. I didn't want to miss the conversation, so I busied myself cleaning up the empty plates and carrying them to the kitchen. Uncle George said to Papa, "Listen, James, thank you for inviting us to the party. I just wanted to let you know that Aunt Betty wrote a note to Andrea in her graduation card saying she wanted to make Andrea's wedding dress and veil. Now I guess she can't do that. You know that Betty has told Andrea for years she would make her dress when she got married."

Papa responded, "How very nice of you both. Betty is such a talented seamstress. What a nice gift for you to offer."

George continued, "I guess now though that won't be needed, so maybe Betty can make the cake for the wedding. My wife is not only a great seamstress but is also a great baker."

"Thanks, George, that is more than generous of you. I will be talking with Andrea about this wedding yet tonight and tomorrow." Papa stressed the word *"this"* by raising his voice. This was going to be a tense few days in our house.

When everyone else had left, and only our family and Jesse and his parents remained, Mama encouraged everyone to sit down in our living room, while I continued to clean up the dining room and kitchen. "How wonderful of you to come to our home, Mr. and Mrs. Payton. I know it isn't what you are used to, but we do the best we can."

Mrs. Payton touched her beautifully coiffed hairdo that was done in a beehive and looked like it had a half gallon of hairspray on it, "Oh, your home is very, how shall I say it, cozy and is so neat. Andrea says she works hard to keep it clean."

"Oh that, she does," Mama continued. "I just don't know what I will do without her." She then lowered her voice, thinking I couldn't hear the conversation from the dining room where I was at this time, going between there and the kitchen. "You know, Patrice, her little sister, is messy and can't clean well. I'll have to redo all the cleaning she did tonight."

Papa changed the subject, "Mr. and Mrs. Payton, that was very generous of you to give Andrea money for her wedding dress, but I am afraid we just can't accept it."

Andrea sat up on the couch where she was sitting with Jesse and his parents. "What do you mean, Papa? I have a dress picked out." She turned and smiled at the Payton's. "This means so much to me."

"Well, your gift from Aunt Betty and Uncle George is that Aunt Betty is going to make your dress because she has always promised you that."

Jesse's mother leaned forward on the couch, "Oh dear, that just can't be."

"And why not, Mrs. Payton?" Papa frowned.

Mrs. Payton looked at her husband and Jesse for their support. Mr. Payton answered, "Well, this is sure an awkward situation for all of us."

Mama chimed in on the conversation, "What do you mean awkward? My sister, Betty, can do something else for the wedding."

"Under the circumstances, is that a good idea?" Mrs. Payton said. "Considering what they did to poor

Andrea." Mrs. Payton patted Andrea on the knee. "Frankly, I am surprised that they were even here tonight."

"Why shouldn't they be?" Papa asked. "They're family."

Mr. Payton cleared his throat. "Andrea has told us all about how George, how shall I say this, molested her."

Chapter Nineteen

Graduation night, 1965

I could only imagine the shock that had to have been on Papa's face when the Paytons made such a nasty accusation about Uncle George. I thought I knew the meaning of molest but wasn't sure and would look it up in my dictionary when I went back to my room.

The Paytons must have sensed the tension that they had created tonight. Mr. Payton spoke up, " Well, we really must be going. Thanks for inviting us to this party. Jesse, it's time for you to come on home."

"Sure, Pop, you and Mom go ahead, and I want to say bye to Andrea. I'll be along in a few minutes."

"Yes, Jesse, good idea. We need to talk with our daughter," Papa spoke up.

"Oh, I want to go for a ride with Jesse. Can I, Mama?"

"No, you can't, young lady," Papa said.

"Your father is right. You are going to stay here with us. We have to talk. Go out on the porch and say goodnight to Jesse and come right back in here," Mama spoke up. I thought to myself that this was one of the first times I had ever heard Mama back Papa's orders.

Andrea responded in a pouty tone. "Well, okay, come on, Jesse. After all we can talk more about our wedding plans tomorrow." I could just imagine Andrea's hidden anger that she didn't get her way, but she couldn't show her true colors to Mr. and Mrs. Payton. I wondered whether Jesse had witnessed her anger yet. Of course, they had only been dating a few weeks. He couldn't possibly know what Andrea was really like.

When the house was quiet, Papa came out to the kitchen where I was cleaning up as well as I could. "Patrice, bless your heart for cleaning up here. You've had a long day. Why don't you go to your room and get ready for bed? I'll see you at breakfast." He gave me a brief hug.

I clung to him. It had been a hard day and I was tired and confused and still sad when I thought that Mama hadn't really wanted me. "Good night, Papa."

As I went back in the living room, I saw Mama sitting in her favorite chair looking pensive and sad. "Good night, Mama, see you tomorrow."

She didn't look up to make eye contact with me but said in a quiet voice, "Good night."

I went to my room, got my pajamas on, and then went in the bathroom to brush my teeth. I was eager to look the word molest up in the dictionary. I heard Papa say to Mama, "I'm giving Andrea five more minutes to get herself back in this house, or I'm going to go out there and drag her back in here."

All I heard was "I understand."

As he promised, I heard the sound of Papa's footsteps going to the front door. He must have opened the door and I heard him say, "Andrea, your time with Jesse is up. Get back in this house."

I heard Andrea close the door and say in a loud voice, "Mama, how could he humiliate me in front of my fiancé?"

"Sit down, Andrea, and you just listen. How dare you bring up a private family matter in front of strangers!"

"They're not strangers. They're going to be my in-laws and they have a right to know how I was mistreated and abused by Uncle George."

I heard Papa raise his voice. "You chose to tell strangers rather than tell your own Mother and Father. What do you think you're doing? If something happened with Uncle George, why didn't you tell us, rather than airing such a statement to those people?"

Andrea started sobbing. I thought my sister was pulling out her drama tactics. She knew when to turn on the tears to her advantage. She sniffed, "I did tell Mama."

Chapter Twenty

Spring, 1965

"Is this true?" Papa asked Mama. "Did you know and didn't tell me?"

"Young lady, you told me that Uncle George patted you on the bottom. You never said he molested you," Mama answered.

I was in bed with my dictionary and looked up the definition of molest. I was shocked. It was more than patting someone on the bottom. I wondered whether Andrea had really been molested or did she make this up to get some attention.

Was this why Mama wouldn't let me, or Andrea go to Aunt Betty and Uncle George's alone?

"Mama," Andrea sniffled through the fake tears that I figured she was producing. "He was always looking at me like he wanted to do something to me. He had that creepy smile."

I heard Papa ask, "Andrea, I am asking you what Uncle George actually did to you?"

"I told you, Papa, he touched me on my rear."

"And what else did he do, Andrea?" Mama asked.

"Well," Andrea paused. "Isn't that enough? He touched me."

Papa turned to Mama, "Annie, call Aunt Betty and Uncle George and tell them to come over here. If Uncle George has done something to Andrea, we need to have him tell us what he did."

"Oh, Papa, that isn't necessary. Let's just drop it. He shouldn't have touched me."

"How many times did this happen, Andrea? You only told me about one time," Mama questioned.

"Only once, that's all. He kind of, you know, brushed up against me."

"Did he touch you anywhere else or try to take your clothes off?" Papa asked.

"Oh no." Andrea responded. "Let's just drop it."

Mama spoke up, "No, Andrea, we are not just going to drop it. What you told those strangers is very serious. You said Uncle George molested you. That's very serious and that is my sister's husband you accused."

"Well, maybe he just bumped into me one day in the kitchen."

Chapter Twenty-one

Spring, 1965

"Andrea, you lied to those strangers about our family, and to think you hurt my relationship with my sister and brother-in-law." I heard Mama scolding her.

"Now, Andrea, you are going to fix this mess with Jesse's parents," Papa ordered.

"What do you want me to do, Papa? I didn't mean anything by it."

"You hurt a lot of people doing what you did. Not to mention you conned your future in-laws into buying you a wedding dress," Papa paused. "Tomorrow night you will ask Jesse's parents over here and tell them the truth and return the money for the dress. Your aunt will make it."

"I can't do that. Mama, you know that. I absolutely refuse to do such a thing."

"Well, Andrea, you'll do it or there isn't going to be any wedding with Jesse." This was Mama's voice. I couldn't believe what she was saying.

"That's right, Andrea, you will do what your mother and I say and will not argue anymore."

"Oh no, I won't. You can't make me." Andrea yelled and slammed the door to her bedroom.

I'll never forget that night. Mama stood up to Andrea. She supported Papa. What would happen next?

I would find out the next day. Andrea wasn't at breakfast. Mama, Papa, and I ate our oatmeal in silence. Papa went off to work and I went to school. We only had three days of school left. I was excited for summer and wondered what would happen with the wedding. I figured I would be sent to my room tonight when Jesse's parents came over.

"Mama, I'm home." I said as I came in the house after school. I went in the kitchen to get some water and cookies. Mama was cooking dinner. "It smells good. What are we having?" I paused. "Is Andrea home?"

"Mama replied. "No, she isn't. I guess she's with Jesse. She left around ten this morning. She didn't go to school. Go get washed up for dinner. It's pot roast night."

Andrea didn't come home for dinner. Papa asked Mama whether they should call Jesse's parents to see if they were coming over tonight. I wondered whether Andrea had even told them to come.

"Do you think we should?" Mama asked. "I made a cake to serve them. I know it will be tense. Andrea has really embarrassed us this time."

"Let's wait awhile to call. I hope they show up." Papa answered.

By the time seven o'clock came, Andrea wasn't home, and Jesse and his parents hadn't shown up. We were sitting in the living room and watching TV. Mama looked at Papa, "I'm going to call."

"Yes, it's time we found out what's going on," Papa said.

Mama dialed the phone that hung on the wall. It was bright red, and I thought it was so cool we had a bright colored phone. "Hi, Mrs. Payton. I just wanted to find out whether Andrea invited you and your husband over here tonight." There was a pause as Mama listened. "Oh, I see. No, they're not here. If you hear from Andrea, please let us know."

Papa asked, "Well, what did they say?"

Mama answered. "They thought Andrea and Jesse were over here. They haven't seen them since before lunch. They didn't know anything about coming over here."

I knew Mama and Papa were worried by the frowns that were on their faces. I figured Andrea and Jesse were probably riding around in his car. By nine o'clock, we still had not seen or heard from Andrea. Mama reminded me it was time to go to bed.

I went in the bathroom to brush my teeth and put my pajamas on. I went in my room, got settled in bed, and picked up my latest Nancy Drew mystery. That was something good that Andrea had done for me. She had given me her collection of all the Nancy Drews. She told me she had outgrown them and preferred romance. I was almost finished with my book when I heard the phone ring.

Mama answered with her friendly hello. She probably thought it was Andrea checking in, or maybe it was her sister wanting to talk about making the wedding dress.

There was silence for a short while and then I heard Mama say, “Oh no, they did what?” Another pause. Mama’s voice went up a notch, “Now just a minute, this is not our fault. Your son should have done no such thing.” Another pause. “You have said enough, Mrs. Payton, good night.”

I heard Mama crying.

“What is it, Annie?” Papa asked.

Through her sobbing, Mama answered. “Jesse and Andrea have eloped. Andrea told Jesse’s parents we wouldn’t pay for her wedding.”

Chapter Twenty-two

Summer, 1965

"Where are Andrea and Jesse going to live?" I asked one night at the dinner table. There seemed to be a sad mood in our house, but I had to admit that I was enjoying the peace and quiet without my sister being around. Andrea and Jesse had been gone a week and I had overheard bits and pieces of what was happening.

I had heard from phone conversations between Papa and Jesse's father that his parents had given them a honeymoon to Florida for two weeks. I had always wanted to go to Florida, but a vacation like that was very expensive. I was sure Andrea was loving it. Instead of paying for the wedding dress if there would have been a big wedding, Jesse's parents bought Andrea a whole new wardrobe.

Mama looked so sad, "Patrice, I don't want to talk about this. My sweet Andrea is gone."

Papa looked at Mama. "She has a right to know what's going on. I know how tough this is." Papa then turned his eyes toward me. "When Andrea and Jesse get back from their honeymoon, they are going to live with Jesse's parents until it is time for Jesse to move to Connecticut to go to school."

"Will we ever see her again?" I asked. "Can I have her room?"

Mama spoke up, "Patrice, you ask too many questions. I'm sure that when Andrea gets back from her wonderful honeymoon, she will be coming over here many times to get her things to take with her when they move away." She paused and started sniffling, "Oh, James, I can't believe Andrea is moving so far away from us when Jesse goes to school."

"It's a new opportunity for Andrea, but it's going to be a big adjustment. We need to talk to her about how she'll need to be supportive of her new husband. After all, he'll have to study hard to get good grades at that fancy school he's going to," Papa answered.

"I just can't bear to think about it." Mama sniffled some more and got up to clear the table. "I made chocolate cake for dessert. I need to get it."

"I can help, Mama." I spoke up.

"No, Patrice, I need Andrea. She always helped me." Mama answered. I was hurt but understood that Mama had to miss Andrea. I knew I couldn't fill that void.

The phone rang. Mama came out of the kitchen and looked at Papa. Who would answer the phone? The conversations that resulted from talking on our bright red phone had not been pleasant between Jesse's family and ours. Mama couldn't talk to them without crying, so Papa had been taking any calls that came in.

Papa said, "I'll take the call." It was Aunt Betty. I heard Papa say, "Sure, we'd love to see you both. Come over anytime this evening. Annie made chocolate cake, so we'll wait to eat it with you." Papa paused. "See you in a little while."

"Wonder why they're coming over tonight?" Mama said.

"They said there was something they wanted to talk to us about," Papa answered.

We were soon to find out. I would usually be told to go to my room to do my homework, but since it was summer break, and we could see the outside light a lot longer, I could join our company. I answered the door. I was glad we could see Aunt Betty and Uncle George more now.

Aunt Betty gave me a hug. "Patrice, you're growing up so fast."

Mama asked Aunt Betty and Uncle George to join us at the dining room table. "Glad you came over tonight. I made cake and I have coffee brewing." Aunt Betty and Uncle George sat down. Mama frowned as Aunt Betty sat down. "Is there something wrong, Annie?"

Mama began sobbing. "It's just, it's just, you're sitting in my Andrea's chair."

"I'm so sorry; let me move, Annie."

"Here you can sit in my chair, Aunt Betty, I'll go get another chair and pull it up to the table." I answered.

"Thank you, Patrice. That's very thoughtful of you," Papa said.

Uncle George seemed to want to say something but stammered. "Well, uh, Andrea is actually the reason we came over tonight."

"Oh, is everything okay?" Mama asked. "Do you know something?"

Uncle George asked, "Have you spoken to Andrea since she's been gone?"

Papa answered, "No, we've not heard from her, I'm sorry to say. Why do you ask?"

Aunt Betty answered, "Well, we don't know how to say this, but Andrea called us this afternoon. It took us by surprise."

"How come she called you?" Mama had a hurt look on her face.

Uncle George answered, "Andrea wants to extend their honeymoon for another week but apparently Jesse and his parents don't want to do that. They want him back home, and Jesse wants to come back home too."

Mama spoke up, "Well, I'm sure Andrea is having such a good time if she wants to stay longer. She has always wanted to go to Florida. It's a dream come true for her."

Papa had a frown on his face like he didn't want to know where the conversation was going. "What did Andrea want?"

Aunt Betty answered, "Well you know how I was going to make her wedding dress as a gift?"

Mama nodded her head, "Yes, that was so nice of you. I wanted that so much."

I spoke up, "Aunt Betty, you can make my dress when I get married?"

Mama frowned at me. Aunt Betty answered, "I sure will, Patrice, and it will be the most beautiful dress you have ever seen."

George changed the conversation, "Because Aunt Betty was going to make Andrea's dress and didn't get to, Andrea asked that we pay for another week of the Florida vacation."

Chapter Twenty-three

Fall, 1969

Andrea didn't get her honeymoon extended that summer over four years ago, and I thought that was the beginning of the problems that she would have with her marriage to Jesse. I didn't know much about marriage but thought you would have to compromise to make your partner happy. That was hard for Andrea. She would call Mama in the evenings and must have been complaining about Jesse. I would hear Mama answer, "You have to stay with your husband. You have to do what he wants—he's your husband." Mama and Papa didn't talk about what was happening around me, but I was in high school now and picked up conversations not meant for my ears.

I never got Andrea's room. Mama may have had a premonition that Andrea would come back home, but I did get her desk. I was a good student and studied a lot, and Papa felt I needed the desk.

We were living in tumultuous times. There were riots at some of the Universities. Jesse was an activist, and we heard he was marching at his school to protest the war. He was a senior this year, he had a year's internship in the field of business, so it had taken five years for him to graduate. He had announced that he was staying at the

University to get his MBA. Andrea was not happy about that. Jesse's parents had worried that he would be drafted into the Vietnam War, but he had gotten a high number and was never called.

One night at the dinner table, I asked whether Andrea and Jesse were going to stay when Jesse went to graduate school at his same school out east. Papa answered, "Jesse is active in student government and now wants to stay out there. He's ambitious and wants to go on to school also."

"Well, it's time he quit his marching, graduated, and got a job," Mama answered.

"Are we going to get to go to his graduation this spring?" I asked.

"Patrice, there is no way we can afford that kind of trip." Mama frowned.

Papa looked thoughtful. "Maybe his parents will have a party for him here at home and we can go. It will be nice to see Andrea again if they come back for a visit." Papa paused. "You know, Jesse's parents want him to take over the family business eventually."

Andrea and Jesse had only been home twice during the four years. Jesse's parents flew often to see him. They would always call to tell Mama and Papa how things were going. I overheard those phone conversations and a couple of times they had made a visit to try to get

Mama and Papa to tell Andrea to quit spending money and quit complaining about everything.

Andrea never got a job while she was there, and I always wondered what she did all day, except clean. I found out one night when Jesse's parents came over to complain that she was partying a lot when Jesse was trying to study.

Mama continued the dinner conversation, "You know Andrea wants a baby, and she has had to wait four years. You would think that Jesse's parents would love a grandchild, but oh no, they support Jesse being selfish and not thinking about Andrea."

Papa commented, "Jesse has a bright future ahead of him, and I think it's great that he wants to go on to school."

"Humphf, what's he going to be, a permanent student? They need to move back here where he can help his father run the business, and they can start a family. Andrea will make a wonderful mother."

I could only imagine what kind of Mother Andrea would be, and I didn't think wonderful was an accurate description.

"Why doesn't Andrea take some classes? That would give her something to do?" I asked.

Mama responded, "School was never Andrea's thing. She isn't like you. You study way too much."

Papa came to my defense, "Patrice is such a good student. She is going to graduate with honors, I just know that, and before we know it, she will be going away to college herself."

"I don't know how you think we'll pay for that," Mama frowned.

"Mama, I can apply for scholarships, so you and Papa won't have to pay," I chimed in with my solution.

The ring from the bright red phone on the wall sounded. Mama left the table to answer it. Mama whispered that it was Andrea. "Hi, dear, how are you?" "We were just talking about you." There was a pause. "Oh, Andrea, that is wonderful." Tears were in Mama's eyes. "I'm going to be a grandma."

Chapter Twenty-four

Fall, 1969

I got a smile on my face at the thought that I was going to be an aunt. Papa and I continued to eat our dinner while Mama talked on the phone and got all the news from Andrea. We were trying to stay quiet so Mama could hear. She didn't like it when we talked while she was on the phone. Papa whispered, "I'm going to be a grandpa." Our immediate thoughts were those of excitement, but then I became pensive. What kind of mother would Andrea be? Would she beat her baby like she had beaten me? What if her child spit up or made a mess? I wondered if Papa was having the same thoughts because his face had gone from a smile to a frown.

Mama was asking questions about where Andrea and Jesse were going to live and were Jesse's parents excited about the news. She also asked about whether Jesse would now go to graduate school. We were soon to hear the answers when Mama hung up the phone and clapped her hands with excitement. "I can't believe this. This is so wonderful. Andrea is going to be a mother." She paused and looked at Papa, "James, we're going to be grandparents. I'm going to have to start knitting a blanket and we are going to have to get Andrea's room fixed up to make room for the baby."

"Are they going to live here?" I asked.

"Slow down, Annie, and tell us the whole story. Are Jesse and Andrea moving back here? Where will they live? Is Jesse not going to graduate school?" Papa was talking as fast as Mama.

"Of course, he can't go to graduate school now. He's got responsibilities. He's going to be a father," Mama answered as she passed the Spam casserole dish around again. "I'm so excited. I just don't know what to do."

Papa continued, "So tell us, what exactly did Andrea say about their plans? This changes a lot of things."

Mama smiled, "Yes, it does, Andrea said she is so glad to be coming back here to live in town. She said that now there is no way Jesse will be able to go to graduate school."

"Is Jesse upset that he won't be able to go to graduate school now?" I asked. I had learned enough about my brother-in-law to know that he was ambitious and wanted to achieve all he could.

"Well." Mama said as she stood up to clear the table. "Jesse can no longer be selfish. He has a wonderful wife and a baby on the way."

The bright red phone made its noise again. Mama was in the kitchen. Papa and I were sitting at the table talking about my school day. Papa said, "I'll get it." Papa stood up and went to the phone. "Hello." Mama came out of the kitchen. Papa was silent as whoever was on the other end talked. "Yes, I see. Let me check with Annie to see if tonight is okay." Papa put his hand over the phone and asked Mama, "Jesse's parents want to know if it is okay to come over in about a half hour."

"Sure, they probably want to celebrate with us. I can make coffee. Oh wait, let's open a bottle of wine for the occasion."

Papa spoke into the phone again, "Annie says okay. We'll even get out a bottle of wine to celebrate the good news." There was a pause. "Okay, we'll see you in a little while."

"What's the matter, James, you look puzzled." Mama asked.

"Well, yes, Jesse's dad didn't seem excited at all, and he said there was no need to bring out wine."

"That's strange. Maybe they're just still in shock about the good news and want to talk more about it." Mama answered.

We were soon to discover what was happening. Being very punctual, Jesse's parents arrived in just about thirty minutes as promised. Papa greeted them at the door and Mama came out of the kitchen. I was allowed to stay in the discussion. I was now in high school and both Mama and Papa were anticipating a celebratory visit.

"Come in and have a seat. It's good to see you. Guess we are all going to be grandparents," Papa smiled.

Neither of Jesse's parents were smiling which I thought was strange.

Mama greeted them, "So glad you came over. Can I get you some coffee? I've made a fresh pot, or would you rather celebrate with wine? Oh, and I'm also heating up some cherry cobbler. I made it for dinner, but we were too excited to eat it."

Jesse's mother glared at Mama. I thought they always believed that they were better than my parents, and I didn't really care for them, but they were Andrea's in-laws. The last four years had been tough because they were always critical about my sister. I knew first-hand she had lots of problems but thought once in a while they could try to be nice to her. "We really don't want anything, thank you."

"Oh." Mama looked stunned and sat down. "We thought you would want to celebrate the good news about Andrea expecting a baby."

Jesse's father spoke up. "You know that our son wants to go on to school to get his master's degree. This new development is now standing in the way."

Papa's face got red. "New development. It's a baby. Your grandchild. How can you just call it a new development?"

"Well, it's certainly a development, if you don't know for sure that the baby is actually Jesse's." Jesse's mother raised her voice and then I saw tears in her eyes.

"What on earth are you talking about? Of course, Andrea and Jesse are having a baby they made together." Mama spoke up.

"Hummph, Mr. and Mrs. Porter, that's why we came over here. We have reason to believe that this quote baby may not be Jesse's. You know your daughter is out partying a lot."

"Wait just a minute. You're saying that Andrea's baby belongs to someone else? How dare you!" Papa stood up. Mama joined him.

Jesse's parents stood. "We came here to let you know that we intend to find out who the baby really belongs to and, if we find out it's another man's, we are cutting your daughter off any future money that she thinks she's entitled to." They walked toward the door and then turned around and Jesse's father raised his voice. "The next time we see you may be in divorce court. Good night."

Chapter Twenty-five

Fall, 1969

When Jesse's parents left, silence permeated the room. What was supposed to be a celebration of a new baby turned into how I felt when I had to go to a funeral. I wasn't sure what would happen now. What did Jesse's parents mean that they were going to see who the baby belonged to? I didn't understand all of this.

Mama got up and went into the kitchen. Papa sat in his recliner. I knew that this was the time to just sit there and see what happened next. Papa got out of his recliner and went into the kitchen. "Annie, we need to talk. Come in the living room and let's sit down and figure out what to do."

Mama sobbed, "What are we going to do, James?" "What has happened? Why would Jesse's parents believe the baby doesn't belong to their son?"

"I'm just as confused as you are. You need to sit down for a few minutes, and then we're going to call Andrea and get to the bottom of this."

Mama moved into the living room. She picked her handkerchief out of her dress pocket and wiped her tears.

"Patrice, will you do me a favor and finish cleaning up the kitchen so your Mama can rest a minute."

"Sure. Can I get you anything?"

"No dear, just cleaning up will be a big help." Papa sat back down in his recliner as he looked at Mama.

"Annie, I think we have to call Andrea and get to the bottom of this. There is more going on here than we know, and we need to find out what it is." Papa paused. "Do you want to call her or do you want me to?"

I heard Mama sob as she gasped, "I, I'll do it. I know my little girl would not commit adultery. I never have liked Jesse's parents. They run that big manufacturing plant here in town, and they think they own the world. How awful they are." Mama paused a minute and continued, "Give me a few minutes to quit crying and I'll call her." Mama and Papa sat in silence. I kept cleaning the kitchen.

Mama went over to the red phone on the wall and dialed the number for Jesse and Andrea. Jesse answered the phone. Mama asked Jesse how he was and then said, "Is Andrea there?" Jesse must have answered no because Mama asked where she was. Jesse said something and Mama asked again where she was. Mama then responded with, "Well, will you have her call me as soon as she gets home? Oh, how is school going? Do you think you'll move back here now after graduation?" Silence again.

Mama said, "I see. Well, maybe you'll change your mind after the baby is born. Good night, Jesse."

Papa had gotten up and was standing by the phone. "Well, what did Jesse say and where was Andrea? Why wasn't she home?"

I went out to join them and witnessed a very confused and sad look on Mama's face as she answered Papa's question. "Jesse was very polite as he always seems to be, but he said that Andrea was out with her girlfriends." Mama looked at her watch, "It's almost 9 o'clock on the east coast. Why isn't she home with her husband?"

Papa nodded his head, "I think that's a question we need to ask our daughter. I don't like the sound of it. What else did he say?"

"He said that he had no intention of coming back here until he has finished graduate school."

"Oh, well, I guess Andrea will have to stay out there with the baby, and you'll have to go out for a few weeks when the baby is born."

"But, James, then he said he didn't care what Andrea did. She could move back here if she wanted."

"That's a strange thing for a husband to say. You would think he would want his wife with him unless." Papa paused. "Annie, if Andrea doesn't call us back tonight, I want you to call her first thing in the morning."

Andrea never called that night. When I came home the next day from school, I asked Mama whether she had heard from Andrea. The response was a quick "No, I haven't." Mama got her handkerchief out again and started sobbing.

At dinner, we had chicken pot pie. I loved this because Mama made the crust and all the stuff in the pie, but none of us had much of an appetite. I wondered where Andrea could be. After dinner, Papa said, "Annie, we have to call again. What if something has happened to Andrea?"

Papa went over to the phone again. Jesse answered. Papa raised his voice. "Where is our daughter, young man? Do we need to get in the car and drive out there to find out what's going on?"

Jesse must have given an answer, and Papa listened without interrupting. Papa said, "Thanks, Jesse, I am so very sorry. I think that Andrea's mother needs to come out." More silence. Then Papa closed the conversation with, "Well, we'll talk about it and let you know."

"What has happened?" Mama was pacing and drying her tears with her cloth. Papa said, "Annie, calm down and I want you to sit down now so I can tell you something."

Mama sat down at the dining room chair where she usually sat.

Papa put his hand on her shoulder and took her handkerchief and dabbed her eyes. I thought then about how much he loved my mama, even with all her flaws.

He whispered, "Annie, Andrea lost the baby yesterday."

Chapter Twenty-six

Fall, 1969

Mama started crying. My mouth flew open at the shock of this news. Through her gasping, Mama said, "Where is she? Is she in the hospital? We have to go out there, James."

"Jesse said she's at home and okay but is just resting."

"At home?" Mama raised her voice. "She should be in the hospital. She needs me, James. I have to go."

"I understand, Annie, Patrice can stay with your sister, and I'll drive you out there. I agree, she needs her mother at such a sad time." Papa paused. "When I go into work tomorrow, I'll see if I can have a few days of leave to drive you out there."

"Thanks, James, we can maybe leave the day after tomorrow. I'll call my sister and see if Patrice can stay there."

"Can't I go? It won't hurt if I miss a few days of school." I asked.

"No, you need to stay here and keep up with your schoolwork. We'll only be gone a few days." Papa answered.

I hung my head down. I would have liked to travel out East. I had never been very far away from where we lived. I couldn't wait until I got older so I could see the world. "Yes, Papa, I understand."

The next day was a scramble for Mama to pack and Papa to see if he could get off work. I thought in an emergency Papa should be able to leave work. He always said he had vacation coming that he hadn't used. He ended up getting five days off. Mama and Papa talked about driving as far as they could the first day so they could get to Andrea.

Papa made the call the next day to Jesse to tell him that he had gotten off work, and they were leaving the next morning to come and take care of Andrea. I heard Papa say, "We insist, Andrea is sick, and we need to be with her." There was a pause. Papa said, "Jesse, we're coming whether you want us to or not."

When Papa hung up, Mama had a puzzled look on her face. "What is it, James?"

"Well, I am not impressed with my son-in-law about this. He said there was no need to come. Andrea was fine now."

"Oh my, what kind of husband doesn't care anymore about his wife than to say something like that." Mama sniffled. "Doesn't he understand that she just lost a baby that she so wanted. You would think Jesse would be upset that he lost his child."

"I don't get it either, Annie, but let's get a good night's rest so we can leave early in the morning."

My aunt and uncle came over to the house the next morning after Mama and Papa left but before I left for school. They told Mama it would be less disruptive for me if I could stay in my own house, and they would come over and take care of me there. I thought all day about the trip and wondered how far they had gotten that first day. We heard from them when they arrived the next day. I had gotten home from school when the phone rang and heard Papa's voice on the other end. "Patrice, how are you? We just wanted to let you know we made it safe and sound, and Mama is spending some time with your sister."

"How is Andrea doing Papa? Is she in the hospital now?" I imagined that Andrea had to be very sick after losing a baby.

Papa cleared his throat and seemed to want to say something but then changed his mind and replied, "Andrea is okay."

"I bet Jesse was glad to see you and Mama after everything that has happened."

"Oh well, it's hard to tell." Papa paused, "Put your aunt on the phone. Mama wants to talk with her."

My aunt was standing close to where I was talking, trying to eavesdrop on the conversation. I gave her the phone, "Hi, Annie, how is poor Andrea?" There was a pause. "Oh, I see. Well, I'm sure Jesse is upset about the baby. Where are you staying?" Another pause. "Keep us posted. We're fine. Patrice is a joy to be around. If you need to stay a few more days, don't worry about it. Call us tomorrow."

My uncle had been sitting in the living room. "What's up?" "Sounds like they made it safe and sound. Where are they staying?"

"They got a room at a motel close to Jesse and Andrea's apartment. It's strange, they haven't seen Jesse. He must have late afternoon classes."

We didn't hear from Papa and Mama the next night. When I got home the third day they had been gone, my aunt was in Andrea's room cleaning. I thought that was strange. I was soon to find out what was going on. I went into the bedroom and asked my aunt, "What are you doing? We don't clean in here too much. It makes Mama sad."

She looked up at me. "Your Mama and Papa are on their way home."

"Oh good, I guess Andrea is feeling better."

"Not exactly, Patrice, Andrea is coming back with them."

Chapter Twenty-Seven

Fall, 1969

Andrea was coming home. I didn't know how I felt about that. On one hand, she was my sister, on another hand, she always kept our house in turmoil with her drama and wanting everything to be perfect. I had gotten used to her absence and liked the way I had Mama and Papa's attention now. I knew we would return to Andrea's demands. I had figured out from conversations I wasn't supposed to hear how Andrea kept Jesse's life in turmoil. He wanted to go to graduate school. Andrea had her own plans for their life.

I would need to be understanding of Andrea for a while. She had just lost a baby and must be in a lot of physical pain as well as being overcome by sadness. Papa came in the door the next afternoon after I had come home from school, carrying suitcases of Andrea's. Mama came through the door, holding on to Andrea's arm. Mama took Andrea over to the living room couch and Andrea stretched out on it right away and whined. "Patrice, can you get me a blanket. I'm so cold." Andrea whined.

I wondered whether this was a sign of what was to come with Andrea ordering me to get her what she needed. "Sure, Andrea, how do you feel?" I went to get her a blanket from her room.

"Mama, I'm thirsty, can you get me a Coke?"

"Sure. Just let me hang my jacket up and put our suitcase away. Papa will put your suitcases in your room."

"I'm sure I won't be here that long. Jesse will miss me and see that he needs me. He'll come back soon to get me." Andrea pulled the blanket I had brought her up around her neck.

"Don't you worry about that, Sweetie. You can stay here as long as you need to. I'm sure Jesse needs some time to think about you and the baby you both lost. After all, he has to be very sad." Mama tucked Andrea's feet under the blanket.

My aunt and uncle, Betty and George, were still there. Betty came out of the kitchen, "I've made a meatloaf and potatoes for all of you. Andrea, I am so sorry about your baby. We'll just be heading home so you all can spend a quiet dinner together."

Papa commented, "Thanks so much for all you did and for looking after Patrice. We really appreciate it."

Betty and George came over and hugged me. "We just love Patrice. She is a joy to be around."

Right after the door shut, Andrea said, "Yuck, meatloaf sounds terrible to me. They should know my stomach is upset. Mama, can you make me some scrambled eggs?"

"Of course, baby, that will be better for you anyway. The rest of us will eat the meatloaf." Mama said as she headed for the kitchen. "Patrice, will you set the table?"

"Don't bother to set a place for me. I'll just eat my eggs over here on the couch." Andrea smiled.

"We can't eat in the living room. Mama worries that something will spill on the furniture." I answered.

Andrea raised her voice, "Mama, tell Patrice to leave me alone. I don't feel like dealing with her childishness."

"It's okay, Patrice, Andrea has been through so much. We can let her eat in the living room."

It looked like this was a sign of what was to come with Andrea. Our household was going to be in an upheaval. As we ate our dinner, Papa asked how my days had been and what had happened since they had left. "Patrice, how has school been since we've been gone?"

I was excited to share some news I had gotten at school that day. "Papa, the counselor told me about several scholarships that are available that she thinks I should apply for."

Papa smiled, "That's fabulous, Patrice. We will have to get to work on those applications."

From the couch came, "Oh, please, do we have to talk about this now with me suffering like I am. Patrice isn't going to get any of those scholarships anyway. What a waste of time."

On that comment, Papa turned around and glared at Andrea. "Patrice will get a scholarship and we are all going to support her, and that includes you, Andrea, if you're going to stay here."

Andrea pouted, "Mama, don't you want me here? I'm an emotional wreck and I count on you to take care of me."

"Of course, Andrea, we want you to stay as long as you need to. This will always be your home."

Just then the phone rang. Papa got up to answer it, "Yes, Jesse, Andrea is here. She left you a note since you weren't there and told you she was coming home so we could take care of her while she recuperates."

There was a pause while Papa listened to what Jesse was saying. "What? Of course, Andrea was in the hospital. She had just gotten released when we got to your apartment, and she was in a lot of pain. I was surprised you didn't bring her home from the hospital. She said she had to take a cab."

Papa listened again to what Jesse answered. "You have to be wrong, Jesse, and you're not making any sense. Of course, she was in the hospital."

Chapter Twenty-eight

Fall, 1969

Two weeks had now gone by since the time that Mama and Papa brought Andrea home from the apartment she shared with her husband. Andrea had been sure that Jesse would come and beg her to come back home with him but that hadn't happened and after the night when Jesse called and questioned her about the hospital, he had not called again. I will always remember when he called and told Papa that Andrea had not been registered in the hospital. After the phone call, I knew Papa had been very thoughtful before he spoke.

Papa had questioned Andrea and she claimed that she had gone to the university infirmary where Jesse went to school. When Papa had asked her a couple of other questions, she cried out, "Papa, I've been through so much! Can't you just leave me alone?"

Andrea continued to lounge around on the couch every day and evening before she went to bed. I was glad I was in school every day because I was getting tired of seeing her there, doing absolutely nothing and expecting Mama to wait on her hand and foot day in and day out.

I had decided that I would just ignore her as much as I could each time she asked me to get something. I was older now and I had no intention of being her slave. I was busy completing college applications. Each evening, Papa would help me with them, while Mama waited on Andrea.

I was a junior now in high school and was excited about the thought of going to college, especially if Andrea was still going to be living in our home again. I would miss Papa and thought about how wonderful things had been for us when Andrea was living out east while Jesse went to school.

The drama that Andrea caused in our lives continued one night when Mama and Papa had gone over to visit Aunt Betty and Uncle George. Andrea was on the couch again watching some silly show. I was in my room studying. Our doorbell rang. Andrea yelled at me, "Answer the door, Patrice, I'm too weak to get it."

I ignored her for a while, and the bell rang again. So much for me ignoring Andrea. I got up to answer the door and figured it was probably a salesman who I would tell that we didn't need anything and send him on his merry way. When I opened the door, I was greeted with a man who looked to be about twenty-five years old. I just stared at him. He was one of the most gorgeous men I had ever seen. He had dark hair and dreamy eyes. I was familiar with the charms of a sexy man and this man exuded sex.

"Excuse me, I'm here to see Andrea." The tall, handsome man said, moving to try to get in the door.

I blocked the door. He might be good looking, but he was a stranger and not getting into this house.

"I'm sorry. Andrea is ill and can't see any visitors."

"She needs to see me," he answered standing taller than before.

In the background, Andrea, said, "I know him, Patrice. Let him in and go in your room and close the door. I don't need you anymore."

What should I do? I didn't know this guy but obviously Andrea knew him and thought it was safe to let him in. I sure wished Mama and Papa were here to handle this. What was this guy doing here anyway?

"Very well. I'll be in my room." I went in my room and shut the door part way so I could hear what was happening.

"Andrea, honey, what's going on? I have been worried sick about you." In a lower tone of voice, he muttered something like, "You know I'm in love with you."

What was going on? Am I hearing this right? Andrea's married. Who is this guy calling her honey and telling her he loves her?

Andrea answered, "Oh Jim, you know I like you too, but we really have to call this whole thing off. If Jesse finds out, he will be upset. My mama will be home soon and how am I going to explain you to her?"

"Run away with me, Andy, I'll take care of you and the baby. I know that baby is mine and I'll make it right."

"Oh, Jim you don't even have a job. Why would I want to leave Jesse for you?"

"But the baby you're carrying belongs to me too and I have a right to raise it."

"Jim, you were a fabulous distraction for me, and it was great fun, but that's all it was." Andrea paused, "There is no baby anymore."

Chapter Twenty -Nine

I never hated my sister as much as I did that night. When her friend Jim left, Andrea yelled from her constant spot on the couch. "Patrice, come here." I yelled back, "I have studying to do." She responded back: "Well, you might want to come here if you want any of those stupid scholarships."

I wondered what she meant. I got up from my desk chair and came out to the living room. "What do you want?" I glared at her.

"You, Miss Smarty Pants, better not even think of telling Mama and Papa that I had a visitor tonight."

"Why not? What are you ashamed of?" I went over and turned the TV down.

"Turn that back up. I told you that you better not even think of telling anyone about this mystery visitor we had tonight. If I ever hear that you did, I'll see that you never get to go to college, let alone get one of those stupid scholarships, not that you really will anyway."

"What?" I asked. "Just what are you saying."

"You understand since you're supposed to be so smart. There was nobody here tonight and you better remember that, or I will make your life miserable. Do you get what I am saying?"

I walked back toward my room, "Yes, I get what you're doing. Trying to control everybody as usual." I slammed my bedroom door as hard as I could. How dare that witch do this to me? How could I keep this secret? I wanted to go to college, so knew I would have to. I wasn't sure what Andrea could do but didn't want to find out.

When Mama and Papa, came home, I stayed in my room. Salty tears had been streaming from my face and I didn't want anyone to see how upset I was. I heard Mama say to Andrea, "How was your night, sweetie?"

Andrea replied, "Okay, I've just been watching TV."

"Is your sister in her room?"

"I suppose so." Andrea answered.

"Did anyone call?" Papa asked as he removed his jacket and put it on the coat rack by the door.

"No, it's been quiet here." Andrea lied.

How could my sister not tell the truth to Mama and Papa? I didn't understand her, but it reminded me of how vicious and manipulative she really was.

"Why don't I get all of us some ice cream." I heard Mama say as she was probably heading toward the kitchen.

"Sounds good to me." Papa answered as he approached my closed door, "How about you, Patrice?

Doesn't some ice cream sound good after a night of studying?"

My heart was breaking. I loved Papa and how could Andrea be so deceptive. "No, Papa, I better keep studying."

The phone rang. I was sure glad I wasn't out of my room, so I didn't have to answer it. I didn't want any more problems tonight. I couldn't imagine who would be calling anyway.

Mama yelled, "James, will you get the phone while I scoop up our ice cream."

Papa must have answered it because I heard him say hello. He was silent for a while, and then I heard him say. "Just what are you saying my daughter did?" Oh no, was the call about me? Now what?

There was more silence. "Now just listen to me. There must be some misunderstanding about this whole situation. Andrea lost her baby, and you should be as sad as we are rather than making assumptions about what may have happened."

More silence. "Well, that's fine with us. Andrea has been worried why Jesse has never reached out to her. At a time like this, she needs her husband. She does not need to be deserted with everything she has gone through. When is he arriving?" There was a pause. "We'll see him then."

Andrea whined, "Is Jesse coming to beg me to go home with him? It's about time."

"I don't think that's the case, Andrea, and I think you need to tell us just what happened between you and Jesse. That was Jesse's father, and he is telling a different story than you have told us."

Mama said, "What's going on, James? Is Jesse coming to take our Andrea back with him or what? I'm confused."

There was a pause before Papa commented. "Jesse is coming to talk with Andrea. His parents seem to want him to get a divorce."

"What, that young man is more concerned about his studies and graduate school than he is about his poor wife." Mama raised her voice.

"Well," Papa continued, "Jesse says that not only did Andrea not go to the hospital when she lost her baby, but she went to the infirmary and was treated for a cold. What's going on, Andrea? You need to tell us. What happened to your baby?"

Chapter Thirty

Fall, 1969

Andrea never changed her story that she lost the baby, but I wondered what the real story was and who the baby's father would have been. It took a couple of weeks before Jesse came to get Andrea. He called and told her he would be taking her to dinner. It was the first time she would be out of the house.

Mama went to Andrea's door. "You'd better hurry, Andrea. Jesse will be here any minute."

"Just give me five minutes, Mama."

Five minutes turned into twenty and Jesse arrived and had to wait for Andrea for ten minutes. I thought she was being rude, but then I realized that she was manipulating her husband, showing she was in charge.

Papa and I were in the living room to keep Jesse company. Papa and I were on the couch, Mama was in the kitchen, and Jesse was sitting in the rocking chair.

Papa asked, "Jesse, what are your plans? Are you and Andrea moving back here?" "It would be great to have you back."

Jesse rocked a little harder in the chair and twisted his neck a couple of times. I wondered whether he had a tic. "No sir, I'm staying out East. I'm going to law school."

Andrea came out of her room, dressed in a pink sweater and a black pencil thin skirt, with a smile on her face which changed quickly to a scowl when Jesse announced his plans. "We'll be discussing our future. We need to decide together." Andrea continued frowning and then continued. "Jesse, where are you taking me?"

Jesse stood up. I thought he would go over to Andrea and give her a kiss. Instead, he took her by the arm and led her to the door as he answered. "I made a reservation at Sammy's."

"Oh, that noisy place. I don't like their food. Maybe we can go to Tony's."

Mama came out of the kitchen and said, "Have a great time you two."

"No, we're not going to Tony's. Sammy's it is." Jesse opened the door and looked back at Papa. "I'll have her home by ten."

When they left the house, Papa looked at Mama. "Well, it looks like Jesse is going to law school."

I spoke up and asked, "So is Andrea going back with Jesse?"

Mama spoke up, "I wouldn't count on Jesse going to law school. He wants his beautiful wife back, and Andrea will be able to talk him into coming back home and going into business with his father."

Papa answered as he got up from the couch and headed to the kitchen for a cup of coffee. "I wouldn't count on that, Annie. Jesse seems to have his life goals set. I think it will be great if he becomes an attorney." Papa carried his cup of coffee out to the living room and brought Mama one also. I hadn't acquired a taste for the stuff yet and wondered whether I ever would.

Mama answered. "We'll see about that. He loves Andrea so much that he may just do what she wants."

Papa took a sip of his coffee, "I don't know, Annie, he sure didn't seem happy with Andrea tonight. Maybe he is asking for a divorce."

Mama gasped, "Jesse won't do that. They have such a bright future together."

"I'm going to my room. I have a test in the morning in physics that I need to review for and then I'm going to bed. Good night." I headed to my room.

Papa answered, "Good luck on the test. If you need my help, I was always good at physics."

"I never took that class. It would have been way too hard for me. Good night, Patrice. See you in the morning," Mama added.

I ended up studying longer than I thought I would. I heard the door open and then slam.

“Hi, honey, how was your dinner and where did you go?” Mama asked Andrea.

Andrea raised her voice. “We went to that awful Sammy’s. The food was awful.”

Papa chimed in, “Well, I’m sure it was good to discuss your future together. Did you two make any decisions?”

Andrea yelled, “I hate him, he said he is going back out East, and if I want to stay married to him, I will go with him. Oh, Mama, what am I going to do?”

Chapter Thirty-one

Spring, 1970

Andrea ended up going back out East with Jesse. She did a lot of storming around when she was packing, and I figured she was not happy about it. When Jesse picked her up two days after the evening when they went out to dinner, he didn't look so happy himself.

I had heard Mama tell Andrea that she needed to make the marriage work. "You can have more babies with Jesse and have a wonderful life. And Jesse is going to be an attorney, so you will be well taken care of."

Andrea's pouty response was, "Oh Mama, I hate it there. I sit in the apartment all day and Jesse is always in school. I don't think he loves me anymore."

"Oh, Andrea, how can he not love you? You are beautiful and I'm sure he'll get over his pouting and you'll both be happy again."

When Jesse picked her up, I had to admit that I was relieved to get her out of the house. She had been her demanding self, thinking that she should be waited on because she said she had lost her baby.

My junior year was an exciting time for me. I was busy completing applications for college scholarships and hoping I would get one. My grades were good, but I knew that didn't guarantee me a scholarship. I really wanted to go away to a university that was about two hours from home. When the letter of acceptance came one day in the spring of 1970, I was so excited. Mama didn't understand why I wanted to go away to school; she thought the local community college would be just fine.

Papa was so excited for me, "Patrice, what a wonderful opportunity for you and you'll be close enough to home that you can come back when you have breaks." Now that I was accepted, I still had to work to get a scholarship because the tuition at the school was expensive.

When it came time for the prom, I really didn't think any guy would ask me. After all, I didn't have Andrea's beauty. I hadn't dated because I preferred to concentrate on my studies. When Brian Appleton asked me, I was shocked but answered, "Sure, I'll go with you."

When Papa, Mama, and I were sitting at the dining room table eating dinner, Papa asked, as he always did, "How was your day, Patrice?"

I answered as I took the bowl of mashed potatoes from him, "Good. I got asked to the prom."

"Who are you going with?" Mama asked.

"Brian Appleton, he's in my class. He lives over on Oak Street."

"Well, I guess you and Mama will have to go look for a new dress, right, Annie?" Papa added.

"Remember, we have the dress that Andrea wore to her prom junior year when she was on the prom court." Mama answered.

"Annie, it would be nice if Patrice could have her own dress."

"Thanks, Papa, that's okay, I can wear Andrea's old dress. I liked it."

Mama answered, "Patrice, I'll have to do some altering before you can wear it because you are taller than our Andrea and don't have as many curves as your sister has."

I went to the prom that night with Brian and wore Andrea's old dress which I thought looked pretty good on me, considering I always thought I looked plain. The dress reminded me of how mad Andrea was the night of her prom when she wasn't queen. I didn't have to worry about that. I wasn't on the prom court. Even if I got a scholarship, I knew it was going to cost Papa quite a bit of money to send me to school. It was the least I could do to recycle the dress. I had a good time at the prom with Brian and thought he was a good friend to have. He was like me; we served on the school newspaper and both of us were thinking about a career in journalism.

It was a warm May night and Brian had come over and we were sitting on the back porch together. We only needed the screen door tonight, so I heard the phone when it rang. Papa answered and I heard Papa say, "Hi, Andrea, how are you and Jesse doing?" The next thing I heard was Papa saying, "Annie, Andrea's on the phone and wants to talk to you."

Mama had just finished washing the dishes from dinner and wiped her hands on her apron. "Hi, honey, how are you?" There was a pause, "Oh my gosh, this is wonderful. I'm going to be a grandma. When's the baby due? I just knew everything would turn out well for you."

Chapter Thirty-two

Summer, 1970

Things weren't going so well with Andrea's pregnancy. She called Mama every night it seemed with some complaint that her feet were swollen, Jesse didn't love her anymore, she looked ugly, and the list went on and on. In July, Mama talked to Papa and suggested that maybe she ought to go out there to help Andrea. Jesse had decided to take a couple of law classes this summer and was studying at the library, according to Andrea. He wanted to get ahead on classes, rather than being a clerk now. Papa said he could take some vacation time and could stay out there about a week. Mama was pleased.

Papa encouraged me to come with them, but I had taken a job that summer at the newspaper in town and didn't want to miss work. I also didn't really want to spend any time with my sister, listening to her complaining about her aches and pains. I was looking forward to having the house to myself. I loved my parents but found that I liked having alone time. Brian was also working at the newspaper so after work he might want to come over. I was finding that I liked him and enjoyed the time we spent together. I didn't really have any female friends so looked forward to being with Brian and talking about what we wanted to do with our lives.

I wondered whether Mama and Papa would have my aunt and uncle come over and watch me, but Papa announced at dinner. "Patrice, you are very responsible. If you want to, you can stay here by yourself. If you need anything, you can always call your aunt and uncle."

"Thanks, Papa. I would really like that. I won't let you down."

"Patrice, the house better look as good as I leave it. You're not the neatest person in the world and I don't want to come home to a mess," Mama commented.

"Don't worry, Mama, I'll take care of the house."

Mama added, "And if Brian comes over, he better behave himself and I don't want him here after ten o'clock."

"Maybe, eleven over the weekend will be okay." Papa added.

"I'll tell him. I won't do anything wrong."

Mama and Papa left for their trip out East on Saturday morning. I had to work that day at the newspaper covering a story on the upcoming town festival. Brian called and asked if he could come over that night around four but said he had to leave at six because he had something else to do. I wondered what he had planned. When he came over, he kept looking at his watch. I asked him what he was doing. He said he had an appointment and left a little before six.

I thought it was a bit strange and wondered why Brian had never even tried to kiss me. I figured he was just shy. Then I wondered whether I was just not attractive enough for him. I didn't hear from him on Sunday and after church, spent the day reading a book and straightening up the house. On Monday, I went to the newspaper office and was assigned to work on a couple of stories. Brian asked if we could have lunch together, like we usually did.

At lunch, I learned what he had been doing Saturday night. "I had a date with Connie Barker. She's so pretty and smart. I really like her," Brian told me in an excited voice.

I tried not to let my shock show. "Oh, that's nice. Where did you go?"

He proceeded to tell me, but I wasn't focusing. I couldn't believe he was going out with another girl when I thought that we were boyfriend and girlfriend. How could I have been so naïve? After all, he had taken me to the prom. I thought he liked me. I couldn't put up the façade anymore. I was afraid I was going to cry and didn't want Brian to see that. I looked at my watch and pushed my food plate away from me. "Brian, I have to get back to work. You stay here and finish your lunch." I picked up my purse and rushed out of the diner. How could he do this to me? How was I going to work with him the rest of the summer at the newspaper? I vowed I would just stay away from him as much as I could. I made it through the afternoon. At the end of the day, Brian asked if he could come over. "No, I have other plans, Brian. See you tomorrow."

I couldn't wait to get home and have private time. I went to my bedroom and collapsed on my bed and sobbed. How could Brian do that? What kind of a fool did he think I was? He actually told me he had a date with Connie Barker. He was running around on me while giving me the impression he liked me.

Then I thought about it. He was just like Andrea. She was married to Jesse but seeing someone else on the side. Well, that was not going to happen to me. I was not going to date anyone who was anything like my sister.

Chapter Thirty-three

Summer and Fall, 1970

I sobbed into my pillow that night over Brian but then woke up early the next morning and decided that no guy was going to interfere with my goals. He was not worth the heartache. I went to work the next day and spoke to Brian but then went about my work. When he asked me if we were having lunch that day, I let him know that I had other things planned and from then on wanted to concentrate on my reporting for the paper. He seemed confused about why I wouldn't have lunch, and I really don't think he realized he had hurt me. I figured it was better for me to know what kind of person he was before I kept letting him be my friend. I was independent and didn't need him.

Early in the fall I was notified that I had gotten a full-ride scholarship. The night I got the letter, I read it to Papa at the dinner table. Mama had been very preoccupied with Andrea's pregnancy so I didn't think she would be too interested. Papa said, "Oh Patrice, I knew you would get some money, but had no idea you would get a scholarship that covered all your tuition."

Mama joined in the conversation. "Well, you're going to have to go back and forth so how do you think you're going to do that. That University is two hours away."

Papa answered, "We'll figure it out."

"You don't understand," I added after I took a gulp of my iced tea. I wished that Mama would be excited for me, rather than looking on the negative side. "This scholarship covers everything, room, board and books. I can live on campus."

Mama started cleaning up the table, "I don't know why you want to go away to college, Patrice. Just get a job and you can live here at home."

"I want to become a journalist and a writer, maybe even write a book someday. I want to go to the University so I can do that."

Papa chimed in as he took a sip of his coffee, "I think it's wonderful. We're behind you one hundred percent, Patrice."

In early December, Andrea had her baby, a son named Andrew. Mama wanted to go to take care of Andrea and her new grandson, but Jesse had other plans. He didn't want Mama to come and told her she could see the baby in the spring when the bad weather was over. One night over the phone, Mama cried and told Jesse she wanted to come. "Who's going to take care of my precious Andrea? There will be too much for her to do." When she got off the phone, Papa asked, "Why doesn't Jesse want you to come. I can't imagine Andrea being able to deal with a new baby by herself. Is Jesse's mother coming?"

Mama sobbed, "No, he said they would be just fine and that he was hiring someone to help Andrea. He thought that was best. What does he know? A daughter needs her mother when she has a baby."

Papa answered, "Well, you can't go where you aren't wanted. I'm sure they will get it all worked out."

That began the calls late in the day from Andrea crying that she couldn't take care of the baby and that Jesse was never home. He was in his second year of law school, so I was sure he was busy.

We had a quiet Christmas that year. My aunt and uncle came over. Mama made her great turkey and dressing with all the trimmings. Halfway through our meal the phone rang. "Merry Christmas, darling," Mama answered. "How is our little Andrew?" There was silence while Andrea must have been talking on the other end. Mama commented, "Now just try rocking him." More silence. "Let Jesse hold him for a while; maybe that will soothe him." Pause. "Oh, I see. Keep rocking him, Honey, and call me back in an hour. You can do it."

My aunt commented, "So glad Andrea called today. I'm sure she misses you. Don't worry. She and Jesse will figure out how to handle little Andrew."

"Well," Mama answered. "Jesse isn't even there, so he sure isn't helping our daughter."

Papa stopped eating and frowned, "Where's Jesse? He can't be studying today. It's Christmas."

Mama sat back down at the dinner table. "He's certainly not studying. He's back here in town, spending Christmas with his family."

Chapter Thirty-four

That Christmas, I knew there were problems again with Jesse and Andrea. How could Jesse go off and leave his wife and new baby at Christmas?

The phone calls came all through the break. Mama kept telling us that Jesse would go back right after Christmas to be with Andrea. That was not to be. On New Year's Eve, Andrea called. Mama was answering the phone most of the time now because the calls tended to be from her daughter. "What are you and Jesse doing for New Year's Eve, Sweetie?" There was a pause. "Oh, well when is he coming back?" There was another pause as Mama was pacing back and forth in the kitchen while gripping her wall phone. "Oh, Honey, I am so sorry you are spending New Year's Eve without Jesse. Hope my little grandson is okay. Happy New Year."

I had been in my bedroom reading a book but had heard the conversation. Papa was in his rocking chair, reading the paper. I came out and asked, "How come Jesse isn't with Andrea for New Year's Eve. How's the baby?"

Mama frowned at me, "Jesse is still here in town and hasn't left to go back to his wife and baby. I just don't get it. Why wouldn't he want to spend New Year's with his wife?"

Papa slammed his newspaper on his lap, "Just when is that young man going back to his wife and our grandson? What is wrong with him, anyway? And what is wrong with his parents. They should be sending him back. That's our little grandson that we haven't even gotten to see because he didn't want us there. Well, I've had enough of this." Papa got out of his rocking chair and headed to the phone.

I wasn't used to seeing Papa this upset but I understood why he would be. Didn't Jesse care to spend the holidays with his new son? What kind of father was he? "What are you going to do, Papa?"

"I'm calling Jesse and going to get to the bottom of this, right now. Annie, what is the phone number?"

Mama got up and went over to the stand by the phone on the wall. It was a little wrought iron stand where she kept the phone books and her little directory of important phone numbers. She had an African violet on it. She opened the little book and showed Papa the number.

"Good evening, is Jesse there?" Pause. "What do you mean he's out with friends while my little girl is home alone with their son. Just what's going on?" Another pause, but this one was longer. "Well, I think he better be making up his mind soon and quite frankly he needs to grow up and take some responsibility. And don't you want to see your own grandson? What kind of grandparents are you anyway?" Papa took a breath. He was on a roll. "And your son wouldn't let us come and help take care of little Andrew." Another long pause. "This is absolutely ridiculous and I'm tired of it. If we have to drive out there and get our little girl and Andrew, that's what we'll do." Another pause. "You'll do no such thing." Papa hung up. His face was red. What a New Year's Eve this was turning out to be.

Papa went back to his chair and collapsed into it. "James, tell me what happened? What did Jesse's parents say?"

"Oh, Annie, you don't want to hear this at all. We need to think about what we're going to do."

"What's happened, James? You're scaring me. Has something happened to the baby? Is Andrew okay?"

"Andrew's fine, Annie. Andrea isn't, that is according to Jesse."

"What wrong with Andrea, Papa? What did they say?"

"They said that our little girl's crazy and that she won't take care of Andrew."

"Of course, she takes care of Andrew. I talk to her every day when that lady who helps take care of him leaves. Andrea says that woman is no help at all and only makes baby Andrew cry more when she gives the baby back to Andrea. He does cry a lot."

Jesse says Andrea is a terrible mother who doesn't even want to be bothered with Andrew. He said that when the nurse, or whatever she is, is there, Andrea leaves and goes out. He figured if he got out of there, Andrea wouldn't have any choice but to take care of her own child.

"I knew I should have gone out there and helped Andrea."

"What could we do? Jesse didn't want us. Now I guess we'll have to go out there."

"Jesse won't want us, James. How are we going to do that?"

"There's more, Annie."

"What do you mean, James? I just don't know what is going on?"

"Oh, Annie, I hate to tell you this, but Jesse has filed for divorce. He says he wants Andrea out of his life. Dealing with Andrea and this baby is just too much for him. He has to finish law school."

"What! He can't do that."

"Well, he's dead serious. We need to go out and get Andrea and the baby and bring them back here. Jesse wants his wife out of his apartment, now."

Chapter Thirty-five

Winter and Spring, 1971

Mama and Papa went to bring Andrea and my new nephew Andrew back to live with us. I was looking forward to having a baby around the house. I hoped that Andrea would mellow out now that she had a son. Those hopes were shattered when the four arrived home. Mama was holding Andrew while Andrea went and checked out her room. "Mama, this room just has to be redecorated. It's too, too.....juvenile. I'm no longer a teenager and can't stand this."

Papa answered, "Now that you'll be here for a while, you'll have plenty of time to redecorate, if you want and we have to make room in there for our little Andrew." He went over and patted the baby's head.

"Oh, surely you don't think I'm going to have Andrew with me in my room. I have to get my rest every night."

Mama answered as she rocked Andrew in her arms, "James, we can put Andrew's crib in our room. Andrea has to be so exhausted after all she's been through."

"We can put his crib in my room, Mama. I won't mind." I put my arms out. "Can I hold Andrew?" Mama passed Andrew to me.

"Patrice, you need to get your studying in. Andrew might keep you up." Papa reached over and touched my arm.

"It'll be okay, Pappa. This is my last semester and I don't have that much studying to do." What pleasure came over me as I held little Andrew. He looked up at me and I thought he smiled at me. I added, "Look Mama, he's smiling at me."

Andrea let out one of her cruel laughs that I had forgotten about since she hadn't lived with us for a while. "Oh, that's just gas. He doesn't care about you." She then turned to Mama, "Can you get his bottle ready?"

"Sure, Honey, while I do that, you probably should check his diaper. He may need to be changed."

"Yuck, I don't like to do that. Jesse hired me some help so I wouldn't have to change diapers most of the time."

"You don't have a nurse here so you can change your own son's diapers." Papa raised his voice.

Andrea whined, "Mama, I'm so tired. I need to rest. Can you feed him and then change his diaper?"

"Of course, Honey, you go in your room and take a nap. Your father can unload Andrew's crib and his other things from the car while Patrice watches him."

That was the beginning of a pattern for our expanded family. Andrea didn't want to assume care for her own son. Mama took care of Andrew and when I would come home from school, I would help. When Andrew cried in the night, I would either get up and rock him or Mama would come in and bring him a bottle. Andrea spent her time on the phone talking to friends or cleaning the house. She did help Mama clean, so Mama had more time to take care of Andrew.

I loved holding the little guy and sometimes at night Papa and I would play patty cake with him and sing to him. Those were happy times that I will never forget. I had bonded with my little nephew and felt so excited to see him, and when he smiled it made my day.

Andrea tried to convince us that Jesse was going to come back soon and tell her he had made a mistake and wanted her back. She bragged that he would never follow through with a divorce. That changed one night in early spring when Jesse called. Papa answered the phone. "Hi, Jesse, where are you?" There was a pause. "Oh, I see, sure you can come over. I know you're eager to see your son and Andrea." Another pause. "Okay, we'll see you in about an hour."

Andrea had overheard the phone conversation. As she helped Mama clear the supper dishes she asked, "Well, what did he say? I bet he's coming to beg me to go home with him." She paused, "He is going to have to do a lot of begging."

Mama picked up the last of the dishes from the table, "Now, Honey, you need to be nice to him. I'm sure he misses you and wants you and his son back with him. He's probably lonely."

We were to find out soon what the purpose of the visit was. When the doorbell rang, I was holding Andrew and Papa went to the door. He was greeted, not just by Jesse but both his parents.

"Come on in. Annie is making coffee for all of us. Patrice, let Jesse hold his son." I walked over to Jesse and said hi and held Andrew out for him to take. Instead, Jesse and his parents ignored our baby and went over and sat down.

When Mama offered coffee, Jesse's father said, "That isn't necessary. This isn't a social call."

Andrea went over and tried to sit next to Jesse on the couch. She was sitting about as close to him as she could be without being on top of him. He got up. Andrea was missing the cues or just playing dumb. "Jesse, I know you want me and Andrew to come back out East with you, but I just don't know. I would have to have help with

Andrew" she paused, "and I don't want you studying so much."

Jesse gave an angry look at Andrea. I kept rocking Andrew back and forth as he cooed. Why didn't his parents want to hold their little grandson? And then the news came out of Jesse's mouth.

"Andrea, I told you I wanted a divorce and here are the papers that you are going to be served officially later, but I want you to have the information now."

"What's this? Oh, Jesse, you're not serious." Andrea opened up the papers she received from him and scowled. "What do you mean, grounds for divorce, adultery. This is ridiculous. You can't do this to me."

Jesse's parents stood up with him. His father said, "Yes, we can. How dare you try to pass this child off as my son's. We'll see you in court and you better have a good lawyer."

Chapter Thirty-six

Spring and Summer, 1971

After that night, things were somber in our home. Andrea spent a lot of the day in her room. Papa had to hire an attorney to deal with the divorce. Papa told Andrea that she better be honest about whether baby Andrew belonged to Jesse or whether there was another man who had fathered this innocent child. I wondered whether it was the same man who had fathered the other baby, that is if there had been another baby before. I kept my mouth shut. Andrea would glare at me because she was afraid that I was going to tell about the night we had a visitor at our house when Andrea had lost her other baby. She never told Papa.

The attorney for Jesse ordered a paternity test. Papa's attorney refused but finally relented. Andrew was not Jesse's baby. Papa was furious. "How could you put us through all of this and never tell us that you were seeing another man? We will settle this because I am not paying one more dime for an attorney to defend you."

Andrea cried, "You just don't understand. You've never understood me. All you care about is Patrice." She grabbed a Kleenex and kept crying, "You don't know what it was like sitting in that apartment all the time while Jesse was off at the library. He just ignored me. What was I supposed to do?"

Papa's face was red. "How dare you tell me it was okay for you to cheat on your husband. I'm finished with you and your lies. No more attorney. You take what you get now, young lady."

Mama had been in the kitchen and was holding Andrew. Andrea said, "Mama, help me. Papa's being mean."

"No Andrea, your father is upset and so am I. You can't cheat on your husband. We can't keep paying for an attorney to defend you when you were wrong." She paused to put Andrew's bottle in his mouth. "You can stay here with us and we'll help you take care of Andrew, but you have to take what you get in this divorce."

Andrea got up and stormed into her room. "I hate you all." She slammed the door.

Andrew started crying. This little guy knew something was wrong.

The divorce became final in July. Andrea got nothing from Jesse. She sulked most of the summer while Mama took care of Andrew. I helped with him every chance I got because I realized I loved this beautiful child who was an innocent victim of Andrea's selfishness. I had graduated from high school as valedictorian and was so proud. Mama and Papa, Andrew, and my aunt and uncle were there. Andrea wouldn't come because she was still sulking.

I had my job at the newspaper that summer. I still ran into Brian but only spoke and tried to avoid him most of the time. He didn't have his girlfriend anymore, but I knew that I would never trust him again.

When August came around, I was getting ready to go to college. I was excited about the new adventure but now I was so attached to baby Andrew, I hated to leave him. I also hated to leave Papa, because I knew the whole divorce with Andrea had been tough on him.

One night I was sitting on the front porch in the swing that Papa had built. This was one of my favorite spots on a summer night. I found the swinging and the fresh air invigorating. I was holding Andrew as he smiled and cooed, so excited to be moving back and forth. Papa came out and joined me while Andrea and Mama were cleaning up the kitchen. "It's beautiful out here tonight, isn't it, Patrice" Papa said as he sat beside me and the baby. "It sure is, Papa. This is my favorite spot. I'm going to miss this when I go away to school."

Papa patted my knee, "But you'll only be two hours away and you can visit whenever you can. We'll take good care of Andrew for you."

"I know, Papa."

We saw a bright blue sports car pull up in front of the house. "I wonder who that could be?" Papa asked. A tall young man got out of the car and started walking up the sidewalk leading to our house. He sure looked familiar.

Wait a minute, it came to me. I had this nagging feeling that I had seen him somewhere before. This was the guy who had come to visit before when Andrea lost her other baby and said that baby was his. I was shocked. Was this baby Andrew's father?

Chapter Thirty-seven

Fall and Winter, 1971

I was soon to find out that this was Jim, the mysterious visitor we had before when Andrea lost the first baby. This guy must have been Andrew's father because for the rest of the summer, he came to visit and took Andrea out almost every night. He seemed to enjoy playing with my little nephew.

I was busy preparing to go away to school. I was sad that I was leaving Papa and Andrew. Mama still did not have a lot of time for me because she was busy with Andrea. Papa was the one who helped me move into my dorm room In August. That was the second hardest good-bye. The first was when I had been holding Andrew before we left, and I had to give him back to Mama. I cried and so did Andrew. When Papa had me settled in my dorm room, he came up and gave me a big hug, "I know, Patrice, you will make us all proud. I'm going to miss you. Don't forget us." He paused and looked at me, "Call us anytime you want."

"I will, Papa, I won't forget you. You know I'll be home for Thanksgiving." After Papa left, I cried. I had tried to keep it together but after I was alone in my dorm room, I realized just how alone I was in a new place with no one I knew. I sat on the bed hugging my new pillow. I hoped my roommate wouldn't be like my sister and be more concerned with her looks than with her studies.

My roommate had not arrived yet. I wondered what her major was. Would we have anything in common? I wanted to be a writer and was a journalism major.

Cecilia arrived about two hours later with her mother. She was majoring in chemistry and was very serious and quiet. She and her mother seemed nice, and I learned that Cecilia lived about three hours away from school. Cecilia's mother asked what my major was. I answered, "I'm in Journalism." There was a pause, and I expected a response like Mama would have given that would remind me I was never going to get a job reporting. "That's wonderful, Patrice, good for you, you know I always wanted to be a writer." Cecilia replied to her mother, "Tell her, you do write, and I love your stories." Cecilia and her mother put her things away. As I watched them, I envied the relationship they appeared to have.

Cecilia and I became good friends. We were serious about our studies and wanted to have quiet time to do our work. Some of the other girls in the dorm wanted to party a lot and loved to bring liquor and even weed into the dorm and were always trying to get us to join them. We wondered how they were keeping their grades up. When mid-term came around, we found out. They were about to flunk out if they didn't start to study. Cecilia and

I tried to help them with work, but it was tough because they were more interested in having fun than hitting the books.

I had called home a few times and Mama would put Andrew on the phone, and he would giggle. Andrea never seemed to be home. When I would ask about her, Mama would say that she was out with Jim for the evening.

"Is Andrea working?" I asked, because I thought it was time that she found a job. She couldn't expect Mama and Papa to take care of her and Andrew without doing something.

"Of course not, Andrea has so many responsibilities with a baby, she couldn't possibly work." Mama paused. "Your father is working overtime to help out."

I had been away from the situation long enough that I could be objective about the situation. "Well, it's about time, Andrea did her part. Papa shouldn't have to work so hard." Right after I said it, I knew I was in trouble.

"Well, you have a lot of room to talk. You're the big shot away at college. What do you know about working?"

I knew the conversation was going nowhere fast. "Mama, I have to get back to studying. Say hi to Papa and I'll see you all soon."

When it was time for Thanksgiving break, I was excited that I was going home and would get to see Papa and Andrew. I left school on Wednesday afternoon after my last class. Papa had gotten me a car so I could come back and forth when I needed. I couldn't wait to get home. It had been over two months since I had been away.

"Anybody home?" I said as I came in the front door.

"In the kitchen, Patrice." "Come out and say hi to your nephew." As I walked out to the kitchen, Andrew almost jumped out of Mama's arms. Andrew flapped his arms. "Da, da," he said.

"No Andrew, this is Patrice, your aunt." Mama looked at me and said, "Andrew is calling everybody Da, da."

"Tice, Tice." He said as I took him from Mama. Tice would become the name Andrew would call me for many years. It was good to be home.

Chapter Thirty-eight

Papa worked late the night before Thanksgiving, but I was excited when he got home around nine. I gave him a big hug. Mama had kept a plate of leftovers for him and we sat down at the dinner table. What fond and not so fond memories I had of that dinner table, and I really missed it when I was away at school. I had put Andrew to bed.

Papa looked at Mama, "Where is Andrea tonight? Out with Jim again?"

She answered, "You know she is. She loves to spend time with her boyfriend."

"I was hoping she would stay home and talk with Patrice."

"Oh, Papa, Andrew called me Tice."

"I bet he was glad to see you. Tell me when your finals are and when will you be home for Christmas?" Papa asked before he took another bite of his meat loaf.

"When I get back to school, I only have two weeks of classes and then finals. I should be home around December fourteenth, and I don't have to go back until January tenth. Oh Papa, I love my school and I have a great roommate, Cecilia. She likes to study as much as I do."

The phone rang, Mama answered it, "Yes, Patrice is here. Just a minute." She whispered to me, "A boy." I wondered who was calling me as I went over to get the phone on the wall. "Oh, hi, Brian, yes, I just got home this afternoon. I love school but am happy to be home." There was a pause. "I see, I'm happy for you if that's what you want. No, I'm going to be busy all the time I'm home with Andrew and Mama and Papa. I'll catch up with you next semester then. Happy Thanksgiving."

"What was that all about, Patrice? Sounds like some nice young man was asking you out and you told him you were busy." Mama stood up to go to the kitchen to get the coffee pot.

Papa answered, "Now Annie, it really isn't any of our business. Patrice is all grown up now. If she doesn't want to tell us, that's okay."

I knew both of them were trying to figure out what was going on. "That was Brian calling. He's transferring to my school next semester and wanted to take me out to talk about it. I have no desire to go out with him. He can talk to me when he comes to school next semester."

"Well, that's not very nice, Patrice. Sounds like he wants to be your boyfriend."

I laughed, "No, Mama, he just wants information, and I'll talk to him when he comes to school. I'm not wasting a night with him."

Papa frowned, "Patrice, sounds like you don't like Brian."

"You could say that Papa, he wasn't very nice to me, and I haven't forgotten it. No way will I get involved with him."

A breeze came in as Andrea and Jim walked through the door. "Oh, when did you get home, Patrice?" Jim gave me a funny look because he was still embarrassed about the very first night he had come to the house. He probably figured that I had heard the conversation when Andrea told him she didn't want him anymore.

"I got here about two this afternoon. Guess what happened. Andrew called me Tice."

"He calls everybody Da, Da, even me. That's probably what he called you. Mama, Jim and I have some wonderful news."

"Sit down and let me get you both some coffee." Mama headed to the kitchen and left Papa and me with Andrea and Jim.

"Jim, where do you live now? I thought you lived out in Connecticut." Going away to school had given me more courage and I knew that Jim had lived out East because that was where he and Andrea met and got together.

Andrea plastered her artificial smile on, "Jim used to live there. That's where we met but when I came back here after what that awful Jesse did to me, Jim knew I needed support, so he came here to live."

"What do you do for a living, Jim?" I was curious.

"Oh, I've finished law school and I am an attorney with Francis and Francis here in town."

"That's nice. Do your parents live here?" I asked.

"My parents are both dead. I only have one sister out East, so I came here to be near my beautiful Andrea." He leaned over and kissed her on the cheek. I tried to see what any guy would see in my sister except her outside beauty. I had to reflect on what my sister had done to her first husband, Jesse.

Mama came back in the room, sat filled coffee cups down in front of both of them, and said, "Well, Andrea, Jim what is your news?"

"Jimmy, you tell them, I am so excited."

Jim paused, "I have asked Andrea to marry me, and I'll build a home for Andrew and my beautiful wife."

Chapter Thirty-nine

Spring, 1973

I loved my college experience but was eager for the end of my second semester sophomore year. I had an internship scheduled that summer with the school's alumni department. I would be helping with press releases for a major fund-raising activity and would also be working on the alumni news bulletin. Along with the good times during these years came memories that were not so pleasant.

Andrea's exploits were taking a toll on Papa. Each time I went home to visit, he seemed older. I had hoped that Andrea's marriage to Jim would bring stability to her life and to Andrew's life. Jim seemed to love his son, but Andrea continued to disengage herself from him. This bothered Papa as Andrea brought Andrew over for Mama's care. Mama thought it was wonderful because she loved taking care of her grandson.

Papa had said many times, "Annie, I know you love Andrew, but his mother should be assuming more of his care. Whenever Andrea wants to go to the country club, it seems that you're taking care of him."

Mama would respond, "But James, it's important for Andrea to keep up with her social life. She has to keep appearances for her husband. Jim is on the fast track at the law firm." Then there were the times when Andrea would get mad at Jim and pack up and come home. When she did, Mama took care of Andrew, and Papa incurred the cost of having two extra mouths to feed.

I continued to avoid Brian my freshman and sophomore years, even though he would seek me out in the library or the student center. I was polite to him but continued to distance myself. I would not trust him again, and I just wanted him to leave me alone. He couldn't seem to take no for an answer. One day late in my sophomore year, Cecilia and I were sitting outside the student center having lunch. Brian approached me asking me to go out again. I said, "No thank you, Brian, I have a lot of studying to do." He walked away with his head down.

Cecilia asked, "Patrice, don't you think it's odd that Brian keeps asking you out, even though you keep saying no."

"That's just Brian, he probably wants to ask me out so he can then dump me again. No way! I learned my lesson from him once."

Cecilia paused, "Still, Patrice, maybe you ought to be reporting him because he just keeps bothering you. I don't think what he's doing is normal."

With a frown on my face, I answered, "You really think so? You think something's wrong with him?"

"Yes, I sure do. I want you to be very careful around him. He gives me a creepy feeling."

"Okay, Cecilia, I'll keep watching him and if he keeps asking me out, I will let our nurse know that he won't leave me alone."

One night late in the semester, I was studying for final exams in my dorm room. Cecilia had gone out to get us a pizza for supper. The resident assistant in our building came to the room and knocked on the door. "Hey, Patrice, can you come down here to the front desk. There is a lady on the phone who wants to talk to you."

I thought that was odd, "Who is it?" as I started walking to the desk with the RA who answered, "She didn't say but she sounded very upset."

When we got down to the front desk, I picked up the face down phone. "Hi, this is Patrice, can I help you?" On the other end, I heard this lady. She sounded like she was crying, "This is Brian's mother. Mrs. Appleton, I know we've never met but since you're Brian's girlfriend, I wanted to call you and see if you could help. Brian talks about you all the time, so I figured he's probably with you in your dorm."

Just then, Cecilia came back carrying our pizza. It smelled wonderful, just like onions and tomatoes. Since I must have had a confused look on my face, Cecilia put the pizza down and looked at me as I shook my head in a no and continued the conversation, "No Mrs. Appleton,

Brian is not with me, and I have to tell you I'm not his girlfriend. I don't know where you got that idea. I haven't seen him for the last couple of weeks."

On the other end of the phone, Mrs. Appleton replied, "Well, he talks about you all the time and just last week said the two of you were getting married."

"What?" My mouth flew open. "I'm not even dating Brian and haven't since he transferred here."

"Young lady, if he is sleeping in your dorm room, you need to tell me. I want to know where my son is. I can't find him."

"I'm sorry, Mrs. Appleton, but I am not sleeping with your son and never have. I'm sorry you can't find him but he's not with me. Have you talked with his dorm supervisor?"

"He's not in his dorm. That's just it; they don't know where he is."

Now I was getting concerned. Where could Brian be? Maybe he was at the library. I had mixed feelings. I was angry at this lady for accusing me of sleeping with her son but, at the same time, felt sorry for her. "Mrs. Appleton, give me your phone number, I'll go over to the library and see if he's there and call you back."

Cecilia looked at me and said, "What's going on?"

"I don't know but I need to go over to the library and see if Brian is there. His mother has been calling him and can't locate him. I'll go check. Save me a piece of pizza."

"Wait a minute. Let me put the pizza in our room and I'm going with you. You know I find that guy very strange."

As we walked in the library, I had a strange feeling that something was wrong. The library had four floors. We started in the basement and no Brian. Lots of other students were there but not him. I was going to look for friends of his but then remembered I really never saw him with a group of guys, and he had told me his roommate didn't like him and stayed away from him. When we got to the top floor, we didn't see him at the usual study tables but when we went back into one of the stacks, we spotted him at a table with his head down. I knew that had to be him because of the blond crew cut he had.

I went over to him, "Brian, what are you doing here? You need to go back to the dorm and call your mom. She's worried." I got no response. Cecilia shook his shoulders and raised her voice. "Brian, wake up. Come on." I repeated what Cecilia said. Still no response. Just then came one of the librarians, "Young ladies, this is a library, keep your voices down."

Cecilia said in a loud voice, feeling I was sure the panic I was feeling, "There's something wrong, we can't get him to wake up."

The librarian became indignant, "Young man, wake up this instance. You cannot sleep in this library." There was no response. By this time, some other students were gathering around to see what was going on. "What's the matter with that guy?" Another one said, "He's probably had too much to drink."

The librarian went over to the phone to make a call. When she came back, I asked, "Who'd you call?"

She answered, "The nurse. She'll be able to tell if he's drunk, and if he is, he'll get thrown out of school."

I said, "I don't think he even drinks." We waited for what seemed to be an eternity. I wondered whether Brian had been drinking.

Cecilia whispered, "I don't like this. I think there's something very wrong with him." She then got very close to his face and looked at the librarian. "I don't smell any liquor on his breath."

The librarian came back with her retort, "Well, what do you know?" I knew that Cecilia as a chemistry major trying to decide whether she wanted to be a doctor had more knowledge than this rude librarian.

When the nurse came, she tried to revive him to no avail. She took his pulse. She looked at some of the students standing around and said, "Help me get him on the floor."

I noticed his pasty color. Cecilia whispered to me, "He looks like he's breathing,"

The nurse looked at the librarian, "He's breathing but call an ambulance right away."

Chapter Forty

Spring, 1973

When the paramedics arrived, one asked who Brian was, to which I replied, "Brian Appleton, he's a sophomore here in journalism." Another one reached into Brian's pockets and yelled at us, "Where's his id?"

Cecilia answered, "We don't know. Patrice got a phone call from his mother asking her where he was, so we came looking for him."

"Are you his girlfriend?" One asked me while the other ones were trying to revive him. "No, I went to high school with him and know him from home."

"Boss, he's got a weak pulse. We need to get him to the hospital ASAP. Everybody, stand back while we get him on the stretcher."

The paramedic who wasn't involved in resuscitating him, said, "Who's his next of kin?" We need to contact them."

"I have his mother's phone number here. Do you want me to call her?" I spoke up.

The paramedic said, "Get her on the phone and let me talk to her."

"She lives about two hours away from here so it will take her awhile to get here."

"Call her now and I need you two to go to his room with this lady and find his identification." The paramedic nodded toward the school nurse. "Do you have his health history? We need to have that right away."

The nurse answered, "Yes, I have his records. I'll go back to the office, get them, and bring them to the hospital."

I called Brian's mother. While I tried to stay calm and not cry, I knew I was on the verge of tears. I relayed to Brian's mother what had happened and where we had found him in the library. I then told her that the paramedics were taking him to the hospital to check him out and asked her to come there. I also explained to her that he didn't have any identification on him. I then put the paramedic on the phone. He was asking whether Brian had any allergies or had ever passed out before. "I'm sorry, ma'am, we'll do the best we can for your son but get here as fast as you can." There was a pause. "Yes, I will tell Patrice that and have her come to the hospital."

He looked at me. I got choked up. I asked him, "Is he going to die?"

"Young lady, I don't know, but his mother asked if you would get his identification and then come to the hospital. I understand you are engaged."

"No sir, there's a misunderstanding. We're not engaged."

Cecilia spoke up, "We'll go to his dorm and get his wallet and then I'll bring Patrice over to the hospital right after that."

The librarian spoke up, "This is my library so what do I need to do?"

"Nothing ma'am. Just have everyone stand back so we can get this young man through on the stretcher." He looked at me with a sad look while the other paramedics were taking Brian away on the stretcher.

The nurse looked at Cecilia. "Will you take Patrice over to his dorm and get his identification? I'll call the dorm ahead and let them know it's okay." She then turned to me, "Patrice, I'm so sorry about this. I know how involved you are with Brian."

I answered, "I did go to high school with him, but we aren't really involved." Her response shocked me, "Oh Patrice, surely you know how much Brian loves you." She paused. "I have to go. I'll meet you at the hospital."

Cecilia and I headed toward Brian's dorm. I looked at her, "What's going on? Why do people think I have a relationship with Brian?"

"I sure don't know, Patrice. This is all so scary."

As we walked across campus, I looked up at the sky that was dark now and it was beginning to thunder. The events that happened, along with the ominous clouds, were an alert for what was to come.

When we arrived at Brian's dorm building, we checked in with the Resident Assistant. "Our nurse called and said I could let you in Brian's room." As we walked down the hall, the RA commented, "His roommate I'm sure is out. He thinks Brian is creepy so stays away as much as he can." He unlocked the door, gave Cecilia the key, and said "Here you go, just bring the key back when you leave." As he opened the door, Cecilia and I both gasped and, feeling faint, I leaned into the wall. The walls on Brian's side of the room were plastered with pictures of me.

Chapter Forty-one

Spring, 1975

After that eventful night when we found Brian unconscious in the library, I felt guilty that I had not seen the warning signs that Brian was troubled. I just thought he was being a pest and, when I admitted it to myself, I had never forgiven him for dumping me for another classmate when we were in high school. Most of the men in my life, especially Papa, were strong and kind at the same time so I was shocked to find that Brian was suffering from depression and paranoia and maybe more that I didn't know about. His mother called to tell me that he was returning home while he got some help and that in the fall, he would enroll in the community college. I vowed to myself; I would proceed with great caution around boys that might ask me out.

One night in our two-bedroom apartment, Cecilia commented, "Can you believe we are graduating in less than two weeks?" Both of us had moved out of the dorm after our sophomore year and had gotten an apartment. Cecilia had been accepted into med school and was moving out East. I had secured a position at a newspaper office as an assistant editor in a town halfway between our college campus and home. I wanted to be closer to home as I continued to watch Papa become more frail. I also wanted to go to graduate school and even though some people thought I should move out East, I just wasn't ready to be that far away from home, Papa, and Andrew. I tried to spend as much time as I could with him as I watched his mother's lack of tolerance for him grow. Andrea and Jim were trying to make a go of their marriage, but their relationship was shaky.

"Patrice, do you know how many people from your family will be coming for our graduation? Mother is planning a dinner after for my family and yours, you know."

"Well, right now, it is supposed to be Mama, Papa, my aunt and uncle, Andrea, Jim, and my little Andrew. I can't wait for you to hear how he is talking away now and is so smart."

Cecilia smiled, "Patrice, I would say you are just a bit biased about that little guy," she paused, "but I have to admit he is adorable. I understand why you want to live close by."

"I'm so excited to have some time to take him for weekends this summer." I felt sad just then as I continued, "Cecilia, you have been such a dear friend to me. Promise me you'll write as much as you can."

"Patrice, I'm not the writer you are, but I'll do my best, and I'm sure going to miss you. You are the sister I never had."

I was touched by that statement, "And you are so much more of a sister to me than Andrea ever has been. I sure wish I could figure out what makes her tick. I'm puzzled by her as well as I am by Brian."

Cecilia responded, "I don't intend to be a psychiatrist, but I know enough about studying mental health in some of my classes that your sister has a significant case of obsessive-compulsive disorder. She wants everything perfect, and life just isn't that way. Too bad she has never been treated."

"We did all have to go to a counselor after that time she left bruises on me, but Andrea always had an excuse for everything she did. She may have obsessive compulsive disorder but she's also an ego maniac as well. Andrea is supposed to be first and foremost in everyone's life."

"Hey, let's talk about some pleasant things. I'm so excited you are getting the outstanding journalism award. I can't wait until one day I pick up your best seller at a bookstore."

I smiled, "Well, wait a minute, what about the science award you are getting and we're both graduating summa cum laude. I think that deserves a toast. Let me break open a bottle of wine."

Our apartment phone rang, Cecilia looked at me and said, "I'll get it. You get the bottle of wine."

"Hello, sure she's right here. We are doing a little celebrating." She whispered, "it's your father."

I sat the bottle of wine and two glasses down on our small kitchen table.

"Hi, Papa, is everything okay? Can't wait to see you." I was silent as I listened to what Papa said. "Well, that's okay, I' m just glad to see all of you. Can't wait." I paused, "How are you feeling?" Another quiet moment for me. "Great, that's good to hear. You know that Cecilia's mother is planning a big dinner celebration for all of us after the ceremony, so I'll let her know."

I hung up the phone and stood silent looking at the phone for a minute before I turned and looked at Cecilia.

"Is everything okay? What are you supposed to let me know?"

I picked up the bottle of wine and started pouring it, "Seems that Andrea has decided that she and Jim should go on a vacation to have their time alone."

"When are they going, although I probably already know?" Cecilia took a sip of her wine.

"Andrea and Jim are going on a second honeymoon the week of our graduation."

Chapter Forty-two

Spring and Summer, 1975

It was a night I will never forget as I walked across the stage to receive my college degree and as I received the special recognition of graduating summa cum laude and being the outstanding journalism student. Everyone dear to me was there and when I admitted it to myself, I was so glad that Andrea had not come. Mama and Papa and Andrew and my aunt and uncle were there. My dear friend, Cecilia, also took honors and was headed off to med school.

The party that Cecilia's parents threw for all of us at the nicest restaurant in town was quite a celebration with many toasts made and promises to keep in touch. I would miss Cecilia, the only close friend I had ever had but I believed we would stay in touch. As Cecilia's mother said, "I want to make a toast to two beautiful ladies who kept their eyes on their goals and have made their families very proud of them, to Cecilia and Patrice, who will make a difference in the world." Cecilia's mother raised her glass, and we all did the same. I thought I saw Papa wipe a tear away from his face.

I proposed a toast then, "To our families, who believed in us and gave us the support we needed along the way." I never felt closer to my father than I did that night. He was the one who had encouraged me, when Mama had diverted her attentions to Andrea. This was my night and one that Andrea would not spoil.

Cecilia was going home for the summer. I was going home for a week before I moved into my new apartment and began my new position as assistant editor at the newspaper an hour away from our home. My goal was to start taking graduate classes at the university in town while I worked. I needed to see how busy my schedule would be in my new position before I made the decision about classes.

I had found a townhouse about three blocks from the newspaper office and Papa helped me move in and we did some decorating. Papa was looking better than he had for a while. One day as we were working in the apartment and Papa was hanging some pictures for me, I asked him how he was feeling, "I'll be okay knowing that you are closer to home and are doing so well." He paused, "I wish Andrea was as goal oriented as you are. I'm hoping that this second honeymoon will help Andrea get her life back together with Jim."

"Let's hope so, Papa, and the fact that they extended their vacation a little longer may be a good sign."

"I hope so, Patrice, although I worry about little Andrew."

"What do you mean Papa?"

"I don't know, the little guy seems so tense when he is around Andrea. She just doesn't seem to like her own son."

"He is such a sweet child and I think Jim does love him, but I agree with you. Andrea doesn't seem to have the time for her own little boy."

That week of moving and getting to spend time with Andrew when we weren't packing things up was delightful. On Wednesday, I told Mama I was going to give her a break and take Andrew to the park. I asked Andrew whether he would like to go play on the swings and ride the merry go round. He jumped up and down, "Yea, Tice, I go and change my clothes."

"It's okay, Andrew. You can wear the clothes you have on and after we play in the park, we'll go get a Dairy Queen. How does that sound?"

Andrew looked down at his clothes and frowned. "Okay, Tice, can I get a buster bar?"

"You sure can, buddy." "Let's go."

It was a beautiful day with the sun shining itself on us. I thought to myself how blessed I was to get to spend this day with Andrew. I pushed him on the swings, and we rode the park's beautiful old merry-go-round together, each of us on our own horse. "Again, Tice," Andrew said each time that the merry-go-round stopped. I had to admit that after three rounds I was getting dizzy, so I suggested we go over to the slide. Andrew was having great fun climbing up to the top of the slide, yelling "Look at me, Tice," and then coming down. On the fourth trip down, he came down a bit too fast, like five-year-olds tend to do, and he slid off the slide into the dirt. He started crying.

"Andrew, are you hurt? Let me look to see if you're okay." He started sobbing. I thought he may have broken a bone. I examined him and moved his arms back and forth as he continued to cry.

"Tell me what hurts?"

He kept sobbing as he answered, "I got dirty."

"That's okay, we'll wash your clothes when we get home."

"No, I'm in trouble."

"You're not, Andrew, it's okay, I'll brush the dirt off, and we'll go to the Dairy Queen."

"No Dairy Queen, I have to be punished."

"I'm not going to punish you Andrew, it was an accident."

He just kept sobbing, "Mommy will be mad. She'll hurt me."

Chapter Forty-three

Summer and Fall, 1975

After that episode with dear Andrew, I knew I had to say something to Andrea when she returned from her "vacation." I didn't look forward to it, but I had to warn her that I did not want her to hurt her son. I was careful that I didn't let Mama and Papa know. Mama would have just denied it and Papa would have become stressed and he didn't need more of that. Right before I left to start my job, I asked Andrea to go to lunch with me and asked Mama if she could watch my nephew so Andrea and I could go out. Mama said, "How wonderful, Patrice, you are trying to spend some time with your sister. I know you've always been jealous of her, after all she is beautiful and has a wonderful family." She paused, "Hopefully someday you'll have the life she has."

I was tired of tolerating Mama fooling herself that Andrea had a marvelous life. "Mama, I have no desire to be like my sister. Come on, you know all her flaws and all the messes she has made. Why would I want to have a life like hers?" I took a deep breath, "I've graduated from college and am getting ready to start a new career."

Mama answered, "Well, I just meant that Andrea has a husband and a beautiful child and lives in a wonderful home and has plenty of money. What else is important?"

"A lot, Mama, and I'm just sorry you can't see that. I'll see you later."

I met Andrea at her country club where she was in her element, making small talk with women who were interested in their beauty and all the local gossip.

"Shall we have a cocktail, Patrice?"

"No, thanks but you go right ahead."

"Well, I certainly don't need permission from you to have a cocktail." When the waiter came, Andrea ordered him, "Please bring me a dry martini, no olive."

We had our lunch while Andrea talked about the wonderful vacation she and Jim had and how they were planning to get away more often.

After lunch was over, I said to my sister, "I'm concerned about Andrew. He is such a sweet boy but sure seems nervous." I was trying to be very careful because if I came right out and asked her whether she was hitting him, she would become very defensive and might take her spite out on my nephew.

"Oh, he can be such a problem child. Boys are so difficult to raise. He's always wanting to get dirty and won't pick up his toys. I simply won't tolerate that."

I responded, "Yes, what's the saying, 'Boys will be boys.' How do you handle him when he gets into trouble?"

"Well, he has to be whipped. I will not tolerate him disobeying me. I have to keep him in line."

I winced when she said the word "whipped." I lowered my voice while I wanted to yell at her because I knew she was probably hurting Andrew. "Andrea, your son is a good little boy. You have to teach him what you want him to do."

Andrea leaned in close to me, "Now you listen to me. Who do you think you are telling me how to raise my son? You're no parent. You have no idea what it's like to be saddled with a little boy. You can't even get yourself a boyfriend."

I leaned closer to Andrea. "I just want you to take good care of your son. He is very precious to me."

My sister scowled and said in a very controlled voice, "Little sister, if you're not careful, I'll not let you ever see your perfect little nephew again."

Chapter Forty-four

Fall, 1978

I was enjoying my career as the assistant editor at the newspaper. It didn't seem possible it had been three years since I had started the position. I was working crazy hours but didn't mind. It was a tough job, but I had learned a lot from the current editor, Ralph, who was getting ready to retire in two years. He had told me he wanted me to move into his position. If I thought my hours were long and involved, I had witnessed him working night and day.

One night I had learned he was out at two in the morning checking out a story that he had tracked for several years about the suspicion of embezzlement at one of the local banks. He had never given up on this story and finally uncovered all the messy details that led to five people being sentenced to prison. He had received a statewide news award for that story.

I had done a lot of follow up on the case and observed the long trials of the individuals. This entire experience had awakened me to the world of corruption. I discovered how much of a sheltered life I had experienced. Our editor had received death threats if he ran the story; he did it anyway.

Once the case was over, my editor asked me if I wanted to be the one to write a book about the case. "Patrice, you're the person to do this."

"What are you talking about? You blew the case open; you should write the book."

He answered, "You're more disciplined and organized than I am, not to mention you're a great writer."

"Ralph, you're the best writer I know."

He put out his cigarette and leaned forward at his desk in his office, papers everywhere. It often drove me up a wall that he was so disorganized, but when he needed something, he knew exactly where it was. "Patrice, I'm not as young as you are and look at this desk; I'm not organized enough. You're the woman for the job and you can list me as second author, but this book is yours."

"I don't know what to say. Tell you what. Give me the weekend and I'll let you know on Monday."

"Sounds fair." Ralph leaned back in his desk chair. "Have you got a big weekend with that guy who's been stopping by here once in a while?" He stopped, "Sorry, Patrice, I'm just being nosy; it's really none of my business."

I laughed, "You mean Bill? Yes, I've gone to dinner with him a few times but that's the end of the story. I don't have time for a relationship."

"Hmm, I think you could make time if you wanted to."

"Maybe so, Ralph," I lowered my voice, "Bill is a bit too controlling and self-centered. He reminds me of my sister."

"Oh, and how is she doing?"

"I'm going to find out this weekend, I'm going home."

"Well, have a good time." Ralph looked at his watch, "Hey, get out of here. It's almost five. Enjoy your time with your family."

"I'm grabbing my bag and leaving. Thanks, Ralph, I'll give you an answer on Monday." I paused at the door. "And thanks for all you've done for me. I'm learning from the best."

"Get goin' before I get all sad."

As I made the hour drive back to my hometown, I thought about Ralph's offer. Could I write a book? How much time would it take? I was working on my master's degree at the university. Would they let me do this project as part of one of my field experiences? I'd check into that.

As I got closer to home, my thoughts turned to Papa. I wanted to see how he was doing. Mama complained he was tired a lot and was worried about

Andrea and Andrew. I remembered back to that lunch I had with Andrea and how I knew then that Andrew was not in a good home environment. By her actions and by what I had seen of the fear in Andrew, I was worried. I had debated with myself about who I could talk to. I couldn't confide in Mama and Papa. Mama would have defended Andrea, just like she had always done, and Papa would become upset.

Right before I had left town to begin my career, I remembered how bothered I was and how I knew I had to talk to Andrea's husband to tell him what I suspected. I stopped by the house on that Saturday. It didn't seem possible that it was three years ago now. I told Jim that I was worried that Andrea was hitting Andrew. I thought that Jim would deny it and defend his wife, but he didn't.

Jim told he that he was watching his wife and had gotten a nanny for Andrew to help out. I remember him confiding in me, "Patrice, I want to make my marriage work and I'm doing my best, but it's tough. I'll do everything I can to protect my son and, you know, he is my son." That talk had helped me a lot and during these last three years, I knew Jim loved his son, and I tried to visit Andrew as much as I could.

My thoughts turned back to reality as I turned the corner on the street where the home I was raised in was. I pulled into the driveway hoping I wasn't too late for dinner.

Papa must have seen me drive in because he came out on the porch and waved. I sensed something was wrong. Papa was smiling but there was an edge to it.

I jumped out of the car, "Hi, Papa, how's it going?"

Papa paused, "Your buddy, Andrew, is here to see you, but I have to tell you something before we go in the house."

"What is it, Papa? Is Mama okay? Are you all right?"

"I'm fine, Patrice, but there's a problem with Andrea."

"Oh no, is she sick?"

"Not at all, Patrice, not at all."

"Well, then what is it?"

"Andrea and Jim are getting a divorce."

Chapter Forty-five

Winter, 1983

"Andrew is just crazy!" Andrea was yelling into the phone at me as I took her call at my office at the newspaper that cold and snowy day.

"What's happened now?" as I took my earring off to hear what my sister was saying. I sat down in my desk chair knowing that this conversation was going to take a while. The snow was coming down harder and I wanted to get home before it got too slick out. Driving in snow and ice was not my favorite thing to do.

I had gotten used to my sister's rants. Since her divorce five years ago from Jim, she would call me when she was having trouble with my nephew. As a result of the divorce, Jim and Andrea shared joint custody, but I knew that Andrew preferred to live with his dad. Andrea had her son during the week and Jim had him on the weekends. Jim had been very good about letting me take my nephew whenever I came home.

During the summer, I had Andrew stay with me a number of times, and I had even taken him with me when I traveled to do book signings and book talks. I loved that time with him, and he seemed to thrive when he was away from his mother. He would confide in me, "Mom never wants to spend time with me and all she ever does when she's home is clean. I don't get it. She has a cleaning lady." Most of the time I would just listen because I didn't want to tear this child's mother down.

Andrea lived in a beautiful home, only about a mile from our homeplace. Jim had given her quite a bit in the divorce settlement because he feared she might fight him being able to see his son. She continued her country club living and all of her social events. When Papa had suggested she might want to get a job, she had become incensed. "A job - there's no need for that. My ex is giving me plenty of money to live on, I saw to that."

"Do you know what that ungrateful child said to me?" Andrea yelled.

"No, tell me what has you so upset?"

"He wants to live with his father, that foolish child." She paused. "And I guess you know his father has some new girlfriend. She's ugly and so messy."

I maintained a calm voice, "Is that what Andrew told you?"

"Yes, when I told him I was tired of his messy room, he yelled that he hated me. Can you imagine saying something so awful to your own mother, after all I have done for that child?"

"Andrea, he's getting older, he's twelve years-old now. His hormones are kicking in and he's more emotional."

"Oh, that's just like you. Defend him. Probably you've talked to Jim. You always side with both of them and Papa. Not to mention, you spoil my son terribly. Just because you have no children and not even a boyfriend, you think you can take my son over. Big shot author. What do you know about raising children?"

Andrea hated it that the book I had written about the bank scandal had sold very well. Many people were interested in reading it because it was hard for people to believe the extent of the embezzlement that had occurred. Once the book had been published, I was trying to juggle my editor job and my public appearances with the book. Andrea believed that the world revolved around her, and when people asked her about me, she resented that I would get any attention.

"Why did you call me if you don't want to listen?" I straightened some things on my desk and then turned my desk chair toward the window. I had been promoted to editor once Ralph had retired. I loved my job but really wanted to go back to school to finish my doctorate. This part time taking classes, along with the job and the book was tough.

"I want you to talk some sense into that child, and I want you to tell Jim to back off having Andrew live with him. He has no business even being there now that Jim is involved with another woman."

"Has this woman moved in with Jim?" I looked down at my nails as I picked off some old polish. I chuckled to myself that Andrea would never approve of me having chipped nails. Andrea wouldn't even go out of the house with one less than perfect nail.

"Not that I know of, but I'm sure she probably sleeps over there."

"Andrea, I really need to run. It's snowing here like crazy. I tell you what, I'll have a talk with Andrew this weekend. I'm coming into town to check on Papa anyway, and I promised I'd take Andrew out for pizza."

"Well, I hope you can talk some sense into my son. See you."

I sat there at my desk, thinking about the turmoil my nephew had to endure with his mother. She expected perfection from him, and when he couldn't deliver that, he would complain to me. He loved it when I took him on my book tours in the summer.

This snow reminded me about how I was eager to see the summer sunshine. Maybe I would take Andrew on a trip to Disney World. He had said he wanted to go there.

I picked up my keys and headed to the door, looking back at my office and all that had happened over the last five years. I had been editor for three years, had my book published and had finished my masters' degree. As I looked at my office and then around to the newsroom, I wondered whether I wanted to keep this work pace up forever.

The snow had piled up on my newest Volkswagen. I had finally bought a new one when I became editor of the paper. The other one had gotten me through college and my first few years of work, but I was excited to have a car with fewer than 200,000 miles on it. I took my snow brush out of the car and swept the car as clean as I could get it. While I did that, I ran the motor to defrost the windows enough so I could see to get home.

When I got back to my apartment, I breathed a sigh of relief. I didn't have to go out at all tonight, so I could get into my jammies and do some reading. I popped a TV dinner into the oven and sat down and listened to the local news, wanting to make sure we hadn't missed any story that they had, and we didn't. Their news was old stuff to me.

I ate my TV dinner still thinking about Andrew and my life. The last guy I had a relationship with was so controlling I finally told him I didn't want to see him again. I had dated an attorney in town, but he wasn't too crazy about the work hours of a newspaper editor so that relationship was not very strong.

I was in the middle of a murder mystery when the phone rang. Thinking it was my "on again, off again" boyfriend, I went over to answer the phone. "Hi, Jim, I was going to call you later tonight to see if I can spend some time with Andrew on Sunday."

I paused while I listened to what Jim was saying. "What, oh my gosh, what can I do? I can't believe it, Andrew overdosed?"

Chapter Forty-six

Winter, 1983

Guilt, sadness, and fear engulfed me as I sat back down in my chair and processed what Andrew's father, Jim, had said to me. My precious nephew had overdosed. Jim didn't know all the details as I thought about how I had given the poor man the third degree about what happened. I wondered why Andrea had not called, had she found him, had she told Mama and Papa, was Andrew going to live. I started sobbing. I couldn't quit. I should have spent more time with him. What could I have done to prevent this from happening?

I jumped up when the next phone call came. It was Papa. "Oh Papa, I'm so sorry. Listen, Jim called me, and I told him as soon as the snowstorm lifted, which I hope will be tomorrow morning, I'll be there." From the other end of the phone, Papa gave me more details. Andrea and Mama were at the hospital and Andrea was being questioned by the Department of Children and Family Services.

I asked, "Why are they questioning Andrea? What did she do?" I was confused and trying to get as much information from Papa as I could but walking the tightrope of caution to make sure I didn't upset him anymore than he was already. I listened to more details as I paced the floor by the phone. "Papa, I'll be there in the morning as soon as I can. If the snow stops and they get the roads cleaned, I should be there by nine." I hung up and just stood there. I needed to make plans, but I was frozen and couldn't move. I was trying to process the whole event.

I went to the kitchen and opened the refrigerator. There was a Fresca. I opened the can and went back to my rocking chair and sat down. I did my best thinking when I rocked in this chair that had been a housewarming gift from my aunt and uncle.

Thoughts of what Papa had told me were coming back. Andrea was being questioned because Andrew had taken pills. The Department of Children and Family Services had been called in to see how he had gotten access to the pills. Had my sister been supervising Andrew? Where was she when this happened? Andrew had been home alone when this happened. His dad, Jim, had been trying to call him back because his son had called him earlier and left a message that he didn't feel good. Jim had been working late and hadn't gotten the message until he got home. When he couldn't reach him, he called Andrea, but she was out with her latest boyfriend who was a pharmacist and didn't call him back. Jim had then driven over to Andrea's place, luckily the door was unlocked, he had gone in, and found Andrew on the bed and he couldn't wake him up. He called an ambulance right away.

Papa had told me that Jim couldn't find Andrea and had called them. They had rushed to the hospital. Mama had tried to call Andrea before they left for the hospital and couldn't reach her daughter and had then called the newest boyfriend. Andrea was with him. I was mad and had contained my anger when Papa was relaying the story. My sister had never accepted her role as a mother. Her beauty and social life were first. My sister was beautiful, but I had learned at an early age, there was a lot more to life. Physical beauty could result in ugly character.

Papa also said they were pumping Andrew's stomach yet tonight to see why he had passed out.

I made a couple of calls to my staff to let them know that I would now be out of the office tomorrow which was Thursday and on Friday. I knew I had to be there to find out what had really taken place and I wanted to console Andrew and my parents. I got into bed, but sleep evaded me most of the night. Why had Andrea left my nephew alone when he didn't feel good?

I was glad my car was in my condo's parking garage because it looked like there was about six inches of snow on the ground when I took my suitcase out to the car and loaded up for the trip. It would take me over the usual hour to get back home because I was going to have to be careful as I drove. The snow was beautiful on the grass areas and just slushy on the road. I took my time; all I needed was to slide in a ditch.

I went directly to the hospital and to my nephew's room. Papa had told me the room that Andrew was going to be taken to after they pumped his stomach. Before I got to the room, I saw Jim walking in the hall. His clothes were wrinkled and his eyes bloodshot. He saw me and rushed toward me and gave me a big hug. When he pulled away, I said, "Jim, how is he? "Is he?" I stumbled on the words I should say, "Is he going to be alright?" Tears were streaming down my face. I knew I should be calm, but I just couldn't take this shock. He hugged me again and then looked at me and said, "He's going to make it, thank God."

Jim continued, "Before you go in the room, I just need to tell you something."

"What is it?"

"My son said he was so sad, he just wanted to feel better, so he took some anti-depressants he found in Andrea's medicine cabinet. He said she always told him that the pills "made her happy."

"What do you mean? He took his mother's pills. I never knew Andrea was on any medicine."

"I didn't either, but I've not been married to her for a while. What was she doing leaving pills out?"

"Oh, Jim, I'm so sorry. Why wasn't she home last night with Andrew?"

"Patrice, he called me when he took the pills and I feel so bad he couldn't get hold of me right away."

"Jim, it's not your fault. Andrea is supposed to take care of him during the week."

"I'm sorry, Patrice, I know she's your sister, but she's not fit to be a mother, and I will do what I have to do to see that my son never lives with her again. You are a better mother to him than my ex-wife has ever been."

The only words that came out of my mouth were, "I understand, Jim, and I am so sorry. I love Andrew so much."

Jim continued, "The Department of Children and Family Services have told me that they won't allow him to be with her anymore. He's my son, and he will live with me. I want you to be the mother he needs."

Chapter Forty-Seven

Spring, 1986

"Cecilia, I can't wait to see you. I need your listening ear and I want to hear everything that is happening in your life." I had called my former roommate, the best friend I had ever had to tell her I was coming to Boston for five days for a national journalism conference. The conference was three days, but I added on two days so I could spend some time with Cecilia. She was now a cardiologist in Boston. She had met a fellow doctor in med school and they had dated off and on and I was hoping it was serious and there might be marriage in her future.

I knew her hours were long and grueling at the hospital and had told her to just sneak away and see me when she could. It had been a year since I had seen her in person, but we talked on the phone a lot.

My life in the romance department had gotten complicated. I had dated one guy when I was editor of the newspaper, but he wanted me to devote more time to him. I wasn't ready for that, so he ended up marrying a woman I likened to my sister, self-centered and not working. When I quit the newspaper to complete my Ph.D. and to spend more time with my nephew, Andrew, I had dated a few guys but there was only one I wanted, and I was in turmoil about what to do. I needed Cecilia's advice.

The first night I was in town in Boston, Cecilia and I were meeting for dinner at the Hilton where I was staying. We wanted a quiet spot where we could catch up, so I had made our reservation and told them we wanted a table toward the back of the restaurant. I had just been seated and was looking at the menu when Cecilia walked in. I saw her immediately and waved her over. As she approached, I thought she had lost some weight. She was a beautiful individual with long dark hair that she pulled back in a bun.

"Cecilia, it's you." She gave me a big hug and then pulled away as she said, "Patrice, you look fabulous. I love your hair. It is striking on you, and you've stayed as skinny as ever." I had frosted my hair with lots of blond highlights to brighten up my mousy brown hair. Unlike Cecilia, I wore mine down.

"Let's celebrate getting together with a drink. Do you still like those cosmopolitans?" Cecilia asked. Cecilia signaled the waiter to come over and ordered both of us a cosmo.

"I sure do and may even have two. I don't have to drive anywhere. So, tell me about your work at the hospital?" I leaned in, "And tell me all the juicy details about Frank, your boyfriend."

"Oh Patrice, life is so complicated with Frank. You know, I think I love him but how can we make it work when we're both working so many hours. I barely get to see him."

"Cecilia, if you really love him, you'll figure out how to make it work. How's the job?"

I listened intently as my former roommate told about her position as a cardiologist at the major hospital in Boston. As I listened, I knew that the head of cardiology position was in her future someday. I knew she also loved Boston and would probably stay here.

We sipped our second cosmopolitan as I thought about how I missed her and enjoyed good ole girl talk. We ordered our dinners and, as we always did when we were in college, we got a chicken dish. Neither one of us were big beef eaters, except for Mama's meatloaf.

"Patrice, out with it. I am dying to know what's happening in your life. Oh, by the way, I found out that you are getting a big award for the series you wrote for the newspaper. I've got a ticket for the banquet."

"Cecilia, that's wonderful." I got a few tears in my eyes that she found out about the award and was going to be there when I received it.

"I want to hear all the details about these two guys you are involved with. Spill it out. Who's going to be the winner, Jim or Matt?"

"Where do I begin? I'm so confused." As I tried to explain my emotions, my mind went back to all of the wonderful times I had spent with Andrew's father after my sister lost custody of her son. Jim had told me he wanted me to be the mother that my sister could never be. I had been very careful to focus my attentions on Andrew and not to think about any relationship with his father. I knew that I had to be careful because my sister would make my life miserable. For three years, I spent a lot of weekends with Andrew and Jim, going out to eat, playing miniature golf. We even went to Disneyland together. I had a separate room, but I found myself more and more attracted to Jim.

"I think I know how you feel about Jim, and I have said for the last two years, you should marry the guy. He supported you all through your doctorate. Now you have a job at the university teaching journalism, your dream job, now go for the dream guy." She paused and took a sip of her cosmo. "Or is he the dream guy now? I want to hear more about this Matt guy. My gosh, Patrice, you have two guys on the string now? I know you're beautiful and intelligent and these guys must be head over heels in love with you, but what are you going to do?"

The conversation halted as the waiter brought our chicken. We were feeling pretty good after two drinks, so we started giggling as we looked at the fancy chicken Kiev we had ordered, a step above the chicken wings we used to get in the dorm. "Patrice, life is good for both of us. Now tell me more about Matt."

I had met Matt at the gym where I worked out, not very far from the college where I had gotten my doctorate and started teaching journalism. Matt also taught at the university in the math department. I had fallen for this guy. He was smart, witty, and I was physically attracted to him, unlike any other guy I had ever met. "Matt is wonderful in so many ways and I have never felt like this about anyone, even Jim who I like to spend time with."

"So, spill it out, Patrice, is there something I'm missing here?" She whispered to me, "Are you sleeping with him, is he good in bed?"

I blushed, "Cecilia, you know me better than that. We've talked about how we would never sleep with someone until we were married.'

"What's the but, then? Out with it."

"He's married."

Chapter Forty-Eight

Spring 1986

Cecilia choked on her cosmo, "He's what?" She leaned in, "You're dating a married man? I can't believe this."

"Just a minute, I am not dating a married man. As soon as I found out he was married, I told him we were through."

"Good for you but you have to tell me the juicy details." Cecilia said but was then interrupted when the waiter came to the table to clear our plates. "Would you ladies like dessert or an after-dinner cocktail?"

"What do you say, Patrice? Do you want dessert?" Cecilia asked me.

"I'll have a Bailey's and Decaf, please." I looked at the waiter.

"Same for me." Cecilia told the waiter and watched him walk away. "Okay, out with it. How did you find out he was married? How did you break it off?"

"Oh, Cecilia, I felt like a fool. I guess everyone knew he was married except me. You know my track record with men isn't good." I shook my head, then continued. "I was having lunch in the faculty dining room with another female professor I know because we are working on a grant." Matt came by the table and said, "Hi," but then he quickly scurried away, which I thought was strange. I thought maybe he would sit down a few minutes."

When he left, my colleague said, "Isn't he the dreamiest looking guy you have ever seen?"

I nodded, "Pretty cute, for sure."

"Too bad he's taken." She said as I thought she was probably talking about him dating me.

"Oh, how do you know that?" I asked.

She answered with a laugh. "He's been married five years."

"Cecilia, I did everything I could to maintain my composure but wanted to run to the restroom and throw up. I couldn't believe it."

"What did you say to her?" Cecilia asked.

"I started packing up what was left of my lunch and told her I had to get to an appointment. On the way back to my office, I stopped at a restroom, went in a stall, closed the door, and started sobbing. I felt like an idiot."

"Oh Patrice, you aren't the first one who has been taken by some fast-talking guy and you won't be the last." Cecilia said, "Did you confront him?"

The waiter came by with our Bailey's and Decafs. After he left, I took a sip and said, "Oh, this is fabulous, just what I need to tell you the rest of this sordid story."

"Patrice, I am so sorry. I wish I could have been there to help you."

"Thanks, Cecilia, but I dealt with it that night. I could barely get through my afternoon class." I then took a sip of my coffee, just reliving that dreadful afternoon was like a shooting knife through my heart. "I went home and just sat there for a while, thinking of what I was going to do. I ate a quart of butter pecan ice cream."

Cecilia laughed, "Always our comfort food. Get out the ice cream."

"I was processing the whole event for the next couple of hours as I corrected some writing papers when the phone rang."

"I can guess who that was." Cecilia took my hand. "I am so sorry."

"Well, you would have been proud of me. It was Matt and he wanted to meet me for dinner. I said sure, give me about an hour." I continued relating the story as I finished my Bailey's. "I went to the coffee shop where we had dinner at many nights. I walked over to the table and he got up to kiss me. I turned away and told him to sit down. At that point, I was disgusted at the sight of him. I told him I had found out he was married, how I didn't appreciate him deceiving me, and said, 'We're done.' and got up and walked out."

"Good for you." Cecilia said as she finished her drink.

"You know, the irony is at that moment I saw him I found him disgusting and wanted to have nothing further to do with him and I have not talked to him since. He's tried to call several times, has stopped by my office and I told him to leave."

"How long ago was this, Patrice?"

"About two weeks ago. I want nothing to do with that jerk."

"Hey, we better get out of here. I've got an early morning and I'm sure your conference sessions begin bright and early." Cecilia went to pick up the tab, but I insisted on paying it. "You're coming to my banquet I feel so honored. The least I can do is buy your dinner."

"I'm so excited about your award. I can't wait to be there." "I'll see you in a couple of days for the big event when you get your honor." We hugged each other and said good-bye.

When I went back to my room, I was feeling so much better, telling Cecilia what had happened. I couldn't admit my errors to many people, but I could with Cecilia. She got me.

The next couple of days were spent in a whirlwind of sessions and refreshment breaks at the conference. It was good to reconnect with some folks I knew from my newspaper days.

When the night of the banquet arrived, I picked a red suit to wear with a white turtleneck under it. I put on my pearl earrings that Mama and Papa had given me when I finished my doctorate. I was a bit sad that they could not come but travel was getting hard for Papa as he aged and had arthritis now. I had to admit I was a bit nervous. I had practiced my acceptance speech several times.

I found my place at the round table that was reserved for award recipients and guests. "Hey there." I heard the voice behind me as Cecilia approached the table and sat down next to me. There were four other people sitting at the table and two other seats vacant. I wondered who the other two award recipients were. "Oh, Cecilia, I am so glad you're here."

"You look beautiful, Patrice, just like the star you are."

Cecilia kept looking around. I said to her, "Is something wrong?" "Are you looking for someone?"

"Oh no, I just like to see who is here before they start the program."

The emcee for the evening announced, "Would everyone please take their seats? We are going to start in about five minutes."

I looked around and saw the biggest crowd in one room I thought I had ever seen. "Oh Cecilia, there must be three thousand people here."

"And two more just walked in." Cecilia said with a smile. I turned to see Jim and my nephew Andrew walk in. I gasped. I started crying I was so overwhelmed.

"Hi, Tice, we made it. I've decided."

"Decided what, Andrew?"

"I want to be a journalist, just like you." I hugged Andrew so hard and then I turned to Jim and hugged him. What a special night. Jim had decided to bring Andrew, 15 years old now, to this banquet. Jim was so thoughtful and caring. I would always have a very special place in my heart for this wonderful man who had put up with my sister as long as he could. We might have gotten together if it wasn't for her. Andrea would have made our life miserable.

We talked during the banquet. I wasn't able to eat much because I was too excited and nervous about giving my acceptance speech. There were about five awards being given that night. Mine was the second one and I was relieved I wouldn't have to wait until the fifth one.

The president of the organization introduced me, told about my award, and asked me to come forward. Andrew and his dad and Cecilia all clapped very loud for me. I walked up to the head table and the podium and opened up my acceptance speech. As I looked out into the sea of guests, I saw him at the back of the room, waving at me. I stared for just a few seconds. At the back of the room was Matt, my ex-boyfriend.

Chapter Forty-nine

Spring, 1988

I was feeling melancholy and uneasy as I looked out my office window at the University. It was a beautiful spring day, full of sunshine and hope for flowers blossoming and trees growing. What was wrong with me? Why couldn't I get over this guy?

On my way back from my last class of the afternoon, I had run into Matt. I had worked to divorce myself of feelings for him. I had vowed I was over him. Why did he have such an impact on me?

My mind wandered. I thought back to that night two years ago when Matt had showed up at the banquet. What an awkward time that had been for me! I had gotten the outstanding news report of the year and it should have been a happy time for me, but life became more complicated with Matt's news that night.

Cecilia had planned a small get together at her home after the awards ceremony and had invited Jim and my nephew Andrew to attend. She hadn't invited Matt because she didn't know he was coming but after the banquet, Matt had come up to our table as we were getting up to leave. I had been distant but polite to him and felt I needed to introduce him to everyone. They greeted him but Jim bristled at him because he was jealous of this guy coming into the picture. I had been careful not to tell Jim about Matt.

We all went to Cecilia's. It was an awkward evening. I was getting tired of being together with both Jim and Matt and said, "Hey, I have really appreciated this evening, but I'm beat and am going back to the hotel. You guys can stay."

Jim had immediately spoken up and said, "Andrew and I are in the same hotel. We can all take a taxi back." Matt had been quick to reply, "I can take her back, I rented a car." I had answered, "No, you all stay. I can get back on my own." Jim became more insistent, "Then, we're going back with you."

I responded, "Okay, if you're sure."

Once I had gotten back to the room, I got out of my powerhouse suit and changed into my jammies and crawled into bed. I was almost asleep when the phone rang. It was Matt. I remembered the conversation well, "Patrice, I have to talk with you." I answered, "Matt, I think it was very nice of you to fly to Boston to see me get my award and I really appreciate it, but we don't have anything to talk about." Matt's answer was a surprise, "I came to see you get the award, but I also came to tell you that I have asked my wife for a divorce. I want to marry you." I was so tired that evening and was surprised at how strong my response was, "Matt, you may be getting a divorce, but we are still through. You deceived me. How could I ever trust you again?" I hung up. I found out that Matt had driven back that next morning. I also heard that his wife was not going to give him a divorce easily and he was going to pay a significant price for his freedom. I wasn't the only one he was interested in and would probably not be the last.

I tried to keep my distance from him, but it was tough because he was on a few university committees I was on. I continued to be uneasy around him but there was still such a physical attraction I had with him, that it was tough. Today I had passed him in the hall, and he stopped to ask me how I was. I made small talk and told him I was fine. He then asked me to go to dinner. I let him know I wouldn't do so, "Matt, we've been through this. I am not going to dinner with you at all. We're through."

"But Patrice, my divorce is final, I can see you openly now."

"Openly has nothing to do with it, I don't want to go out with you. We are finished and have been for a long time." I went right back to my office and there I sat. I just wanted to be over him. I would never trust him again. I needed to seek some happy thoughts now. Papa had retired from his job. It had taken its toll on him. He had serious heart problems and high blood pressure. I worried so about him. He had always been my anchor to happiness. I hadn't told him about Matt. He was perceptive about Jim and continued to ask me whether our relationship was serious. I had been emphatic that it was not, and we were just friends. I would call him. I needed to hear his consoling and accepting voice. I picked up my office phone to call home.

Mama answered the phone, I spent the first three minutes hearing all about Andrea's beautiful home and her boyfriend the pharmacist. She had been dating him for quite a while and I suspected he was living at her house, but he still maintained his own home. I couldn't resist, "Are there any marriage plans in my sister's future?" On that note, Mama wanted to end the conversation. "Can I talk to Papa?" I asked. I heard Mama say in a less than excited tone, "It's Patrice. She wants to talk with you."

"Hi, Papa. Hey, I've got sometime Sunday afternoon and can I drive down to see you and Mama?" I realized just then how much I needed my Papa fix. On the other end, Papa said, "Sure, we're supposed to go over to Jim and Andrew's. I'm sure you can join us." I felt awkward. I didn't want to invite myself over there but did want to see my nephew who was growing up so fast. He was going to go to the college where I graduated, and I was so excited about that. Just like the night of the banquet, he had said he wanted to become a journalist just like his Aunt Tice.

I answered Papa, "Well, let me see about that. I don't want to just invite myself."

Papa said, "Well, we'll see. Maybe we'll invite Jim and Andrew over here for one of mama's fabulous Sunday dinners."

As much as I resented Mama's attentions to Andrea, I loved her cooking. "That sounds good, Papa. I'll see you on Sunday. I can't wait."

I had been right. Talking to Papa on the phone had made me feel better. I stayed at my desk the next three hours catching up with grading my students' papers. I loved teaching journalism at the university. I got home from school around seven, popped a TV dinner in the oven, thinking no wonder I appreciated Mama's cooking, I did so little cooking myself.

The phone rang and I answered to a familiar voice. It was Jim. From the other end of the phone, he said, "Hey, Patrice, I heard you're coming on Sunday afternoon. I'd like to invite you to come over here. I'll cook Sunday dinner."

I laughed, "Oh, I see you talked to Papa."

Jim answered, "Well, not exactly but Andrew talked to him and told him you were coming, so I wanted you to know you were welcome. Actually, Patrice, you are more than welcome. We really need to talk."

My alarm buttons were ringing, "What's wrong, Jim, is Andrew sick? Are you sick?"

Jim laughed, "Oh Patrice, nobody is sick, quit worrying. We're fine, I mean health-wise." Jim's voice tone had changed from happy to serious.

"Well then, what is it Jim?" I was now pacing up and down my dining room floor where the phone was.

"We have to talk, Patrice. I need you."

I frowned, "Are you sure everything is okay with Andrew? What is it you're not telling me?"

"It has nothing to do with Andrew. It's us, you and me. I need you, Patrice, I don't want to go through this friendship stuff anymore."

"Oh Jim, have I done something to upset you. You don't want to be my friend anymore?"

"Patrice, I want us to be much more than just friends. It's time."

Chapter Fifty

Summer, 1988

I loved the summer which gave me time to reflect, rejuvenate, and reconnect. I was only teaching one class, and it was a concentrated two-week long all-day class for journalism majors. The class was intense because students were choosing a story and developing a series of articles about that story. It was great fun for me to see their writing shine. I loved teaching and seeing their progress. I also loved spending the time helping those who were struggling. Life was good in my professional life.

I had gone back to my office at the end of class the last day. I turned in final grades for this seminar and leaned back in my chair. I was leaving for home tomorrow morning to spend a week at Mama and Papa's. Another advantage to summer, I got to spend more time with them as they were aging. Papa had continued to have heart problems and I wanted to watch him more closely. Andrea lived right there, but she never seemed to have the time to spend with our parents

I had tonight all to myself and decided to grab some takeout food and go sit at the lake. I needed to give Jim an answer this weekend. He deserved that much from me. I thought back to the weekend when I had gone home this past spring after he had told me he loved me and wanted to make a life with me. Andrew, my nephew, was going away to college, and Jim had proposed to me. I cried when his words came, "Patrice, I love you and have for many years. I want to spend the rest of my life with you. We only live an hour apart. We can make this work."

"But that's just it, Jim, you are so dear to me," but, I had paused, "Andrea will always be in the middle of our lives."

"I'm tired of Andrea controlling my life and yours. We can't let her do this."

Looking at the peaceful calm water always made me think clearly and that night I had decided. When I got home tomorrow, I would let Jim know my answer.

I finished my sandwich, threw the wrapper away, and got into my Volkswagen. I stopped at our local discount store to pick up some of Mama and Papa's favorite candies to take home tomorrow. I got a new hat for Andrew and bought a book for Jim that I knew he would like.

When I got back to my condo, I saw my phone line blinking with a message. It was from Papa and he sounded distraught. I listened to the message, "Patrice, please call me just as soon as you get home." I tried to call back right away and there was no answer. What was going on? Why wasn't anybody at home. Papa had left the message about an hour ago. What should I do? I tried to call my sister at her home but figured that wouldn't do me any good, because she was probably out on the town with her boyfriend. I paced. I thought, who else can I call? I tried to call my Aunt. There was no answer. Maybe I should call Jim, he might know. I tried his number at home and again met disappointment when I got his answering machine. I thought I was just worrying too much and that I needed to calm down and think about what I should do.

Just then, my doorbell rang. Who could be calling on me at nine at night. I went to the closed door, "Who is it?"

"It's Jim, Patrice."

I opened the door. Jim came in and gave me a big hug. He was tense but tender. He pulled back and looked at me with those loving eyes I had learned to cherish. "Patrice, I came to get you. I didn't want you to drive. Your Mama has been taken to the hospital. They think she had a stroke."

Chapter Fifty-one

Summer, 1988

"Oh, Jim, I can't believe I didn't notice that Mama wasn't feeling well. How could I have missed the signs? I have been so worried about Papa." I was thinking about whether there was any sign that my mother wasn't feeling well. Jim and I were in his car on the way back to my hometown and to the hospital.

"Patrice, many times there are no obvious warning signs for a stroke. Andrew just spent time with your parents a couple of days ago. He didn't say a word about your mother, just said your dad was very tired and had taken a nap during the day which he thought was odd." We had stopped at the light on the outskirts of town and weren't too far from the hospital now. Jim put his hand on my leg. "I'm sure she'll be okay, and I'm here to help you."

I put my hand on top of his and looked at him as he pulled into the hospital parking lot. "Jim, I can't thank you enough for coming to get me. You know, I don't think I could have driven by myself." I paused, "Isn't it funny how you think that your parents will always be around to take care of you and then it slaps you in the face that they may not be."

Jim pulled into a parking place, turned off the motor, and said, "I know how you feel. When my dad died right after I graduated from college, I just couldn't wrap my head around the fact that he was gone. For a couple of years, I would reach for the phone to tell him some business news." Jim got out of the car and came over to open my door. He put his arm around me. "It's going to be okay, Patrice."

I leaned my head into his shoulder. His body felt so warm and comforting to me.

"I sent Andrew home to get some rest. He didn't want to leave his grandma's side. but I told him we would need him in the morning."

"Thanks, Jim, you are a godsend to me."

"You know I always want to be here for you."

Because Jim was a community leader, many people knew him at the local hospital and several people spoke to him and he easily got us access to Mama's room.

As we entered the room, Mama was sleeping, and Papa was sitting in a chair by her bed. He had been dozing. "Papa, are you okay?" I nudged him and said in a whisper. He stood up and gave me the bear hug that I loved so much. "Papa, can you tell me what happened? Sit down." By then Jim had gotten a couple of chairs from the other side of the room. Mama didn't have a roommate so we could have more privacy.

"Your mother finished cooking dinner and was cleaning up the kitchen. She said during dinner that she didn't feel good but couldn't figure out why." Papa hung his head down. "I should have made her go in and rest and I should have cleaned up."

Jim spoke in his calm and soothing voice, "James, you had no way of knowing that this was going to happen to Annie."

"I just can't believe this. Annie has always been healthy. What could have caused her to have a stroke?"

"Sometimes things just can't be explained." I said to Papa as I sat next to him and held his hand. Mama was sleeping and didn't seem to hear anything that was going on.

Andrea walked in or should I say she stormed in and took a look at Jim and blurted. "What is he doing here? He's certainly not family."

I stood up and said, "He brought me here, Andrea, and he is family. He is the father of your son, my nephew."

Jim looked at me and then at Papa and said, "Hey, let's go get you a cup of coffee, James. Patrice, can I bring you a cup also?"

"No thanks but take your time. You and Papa can talk."

Andrea looked at me, "Well, it's about time you got here, Miss Big Shot." She paused, "And I am sick of that ex-husband of mine thinking you're so special." She laughed, "I know he's never gotten over me but to want to spend time with you. Really."

"Will you please hold your voice down, Andrea? Mama is resting."

"Resting, is that what you think. Look at her, she's a vegetable now. They said she had a stroke. She was drooling earlier. Can you imagine?"

"Just because she was drooling does not mean she can't hear and see. Please be quiet."

Andrea's long- term boyfriend, Gregory, walked into the room. He was a pharmacist and thought he was God's gift to the world. He didn't even say hello to me. As he kissed Andrea on the cheek, he said, "Don't worry I've made some calls and when your mother is released from here, I think I have a place that will take her."

Confused, I said, "What are you talking about, a place to take her? When she gets out of here, she'll go home with Papa."

Andrea laughed, "You can't be serious. Neither one of them are going back to that old house."

"Why not?" I said, "I have time off this summer and can help them until Mama gets better."

"Oh sure, you never do anything, and always leave all the work and responsibility of taking care of both of them to me. News flash, Miss Journalism, I can't do it anymore, and I have made a decision."

I was trying to keep from losing my temper, especially when she was saying she had all the responsibility. That was just a lie, but I contained myself. "Andrea, you don't make the decisions. We do and Mama and Papa do."

"That's what you think. I am putting them both in a nursing home. I'll make the deposit tomorrow."

Chapter Fifty-two

Summer, 1988

"Patrice, I don't want Annie and me put in a nursing home. I can take care of my wife here." We had left Mama sleeping at the hospital and planned to be back in the morning. It had been a tense night; made even worse with Andrea's declaration that she was putting Mama and Papa in a nursing home. I had no idea she had made that statement to Papa. I had made it clear that she was going to do no such thing. Greg, Andrea's boyfriend, thought he had all the answers in the medical world because he was a pharmacist.

We were sitting around the dining room table. It seemed strange that Mama wasn't here. She was always at the house and spent most of her time cooking in the kitchen or serving food at our table. I was feeling very sad at that realization that she wouldn't be here tonight.

When we arrived home from the hospital, Jim brought my bags in and insisted that both Papa and I sit down while he brewed some decaf coffee for us. I really didn't have any appetite, but Jim found some cobbler that Mama had made and served us that.

"Papa, you and Mama are not going to a nursing home. Remember I can stay here for the next few weeks and will help you. We can do it."

Jim took a sip of his coffee, "Hey, I can help out this summer and remember our boy, Andrew, is available. He hasn't gone away to college yet. We'll get along just fine."

"I'm sure glad I have you to help. I can manage, but it sure is good to know you're here, Patrice, and thank you, Jim." Papa reached across the table and patted my hand.

"Hey, we'll all work together. We'll probably have to take Mama to therapy and then follow up here at home, but we can do it." I paused as I looked at Papa, "You need to tell me how you're feeling? You look so tired."

"Are you sure you're feeling okay, James?" Jim asked. "Maybe it's none of my business, but Andrew said you seem to fall asleep a lot in your chair."

"Jim, it's so strange, ever since the doctor prescribed that heart medicine for me, I've been more tired than ever before. I thought that medicine would make me feel better, but it doesn't." Papa sighed. "Some days I can barely get out of bed. I was looking forward to retiring, so I could do more work around the house and in the yard, but I can barely get anything done." He shook his head.

"Maybe once Mama gets home from the hospital, I'll make an appointment for you to see the heart specialist again." I paused, "Hmm, Cecilia, my dear friend, is a cardiologist. Maybe I'll ask her for an opinion."

"That's nice, Patrice. I'm so glad you're here. I trust you." Papa took a bite of his cobbler. "Patrice, I have to ask you something."

"Sure, what is it?" I had just put my coffee cup down.

"Will you be the power of attorney for your Mother and me?"

Jim frowned, "James, you don't need a power of attorney right now. You are of sound mind and can take care of you and your wife. You can make medical decisions yourself."

"That's right, Papa. If Mama can't make decisions for herself, you as her husband can make decisions." I leaned forward toward Papa. "Didn't you have to sign papers tonight that you are her next of kin?"

"Yes, I signed some papers." Papa answered.

Jim seemed to read Papa's mind. Even though he wasn't related to my parents, he spent quite a bit of time with them because he brought Andrew over as much as possible. "James, are you worried because of what Andrea said? What exactly did Andrea say to you?"

Papa answered, "Greg and Andrea were talking out in the hall while they thought I was sleeping in the chair in the room. I heard Greg tell Andrea that she needed to take over all the decision making."

I wanted to stay calm but was still seething after Andrea had told me that she was putting both of them in a nursing home. I had thought over my dead body. "Papa, Andrea is not putting you and Mama anywhere. Trust me that won't happen."

"But Patrice, Greg told Andrea that she needed to be our power of attorney and then she can take over, sell the house, put us in the nursing home, and then she'll be free."

Chapter Fifty-three

Summer, 1988

On the drive to the hospital, Papa told me again that he wanted me to be power of attorney. Jim and I had talked about it after Papa went to bed and thought it would be a good idea. We were frightened about what Andrea might do. Jim answered Papa as he turned the corner, "I think you're right, James. Why don't I contact an attorney friend of mine to draw up the paperwork? I can't do it because it would be a conflict of interest."

"Good idea, Jim, thanks for doing that. I'm going to check about the papers that Papa signed yesterday." I answered.

"Thanks, Jim, and Patrice, thanks for being willing to be the power of attorney. You know I trust you with my life." Papa replied.

"Hey, why don't I drop the two of you off at the door? I want to go pick up Andrew." Jim was pulling the car into the hospital drive and approaching the front entrance. "He was sleeping in when I left. On the way back here, I'll buzz over to the attorney's office and meet you back here at the hospital in a couple of hours."

"Thanks, Jim" I turned to him and smiled. He could always cheer me up. I looked in the back seat, "You ready, Papa?"

As we walked through the antiseptic environment, I thought about how I hated hospitals. I remembered when Andrew had taken an overdose. That was one of the scariest days of my life. We were fortunate that Andrew had done much better when his life was stable living with Jim.

When we got in the room, Mama was propped up and had finished her breakfast. She smiled as Papa went over to give her a big hug. "How are you feeling, Annie? You look good."

"I feel okay, but I'm worried, James. I can't feel my left leg or my left arm." She tried to lift her left arm and it was limp.

"Has the doctor been in, Mama?" I asked.

"I don't think so." Mama answered, looking confused.

"Let me go out and check to see what the nurse says. I'll be right back. Papa, you stay here."

I went out to the nurse's station and asked the nurse at the desk, "Can you tell me if the doctor has been in to see Annie Porter this morning?"

"Let me check. Who are you by the way? Are you a relative?"

"Yes, I'm her daughter."

"Oh, we didn't know she had another daughter. Andrea was here last night and took care of things."

"Just what kind of things did my sister take care of? My sister cannot make decisions without my father or me." I was getting irritated and worried. What had my sister done now?

"Well, let me pull her chart. I can tell you she hasn't seen a doctor this morning, but you aren't on the list of family members so I can't divulge any further information."

"Excuse me, I'm her daughter and I do have a right to know."

"I certainly am not going to argue with you, but you do not have a right to know. There were papers signed last night, and they don't mention you."

"Well, let me see those papers right now." I was keeping my voice low, but I was getting angry.

"Miss, I don't intend to argue with you. You can't see any papers. Do you understand? Work this out with your sister and your father. We have laws."

"Just a minute. Let me get my father."

"Very well, whatever." The nurse said as she shrugged and turned away from me as if she had better things to do.

I took a deep breath to calm down before I went into Mama's room. "Papa, can you come out to the front desk with me?"

"Sure, Patrice. Is something wrong?"

"Oh no," I lied. I wanted to scream.

When we got outside the door, Papa looked at me, "What's the matter?"

I looked at Papa, "I just need for you to ask the nurse to see the forms you signed last night."

"Okay, sure Patrice." Papa went over to the nasty nurse and said, "Ma'am, can I see my wife's chart?"

The nurse gave me a dirty look and addressed Papa, "I guess it will be all right."

Papa started reading the papers. He frowned as he looked at the small print. "What does this mean, Patrice, I don't remember signing anything like this?"

Papa handed me the papers. There it was in writing. Papa had signed in the box where it had said, "Please list power of attorney for health purposes for Annie Porter. In the blank it said Andrea Porter and below that line, Papa's signature appeared.

Chapter Fifty-four

Summer of 1988

"There's some mistake." Papa said. "I would remember signing this. I never signed for Andrea to be Annie's power of attorney." He paused and looked at me with an air of desperation. "I know that Andrea's name was not on this piece of paper I signed."

The nurse smirked, "A lot of people don't understand what they are signing when they are under stress."

Papa gave the form to me to look at, "I know what I signed, and this is not it, lady. Don't try to patronize me."

I looked at the sheet again. I was used to investigative journalism and this document looked doctored to me. "Well, it certainly looks like this form has had this added and it is not acceptable. It's going to be changed."

"Well, we'll just see about that." The nurse scowled. "Now, if you'll excuse me, give me back that paper. I have work to do."

"Excuse me. My father has a right to that paper or a copy of it, so I suggest you give him either this form or a copy right now. If we have to bring an attorney to get a copy of the document, we'll do it." I leaned in toward the nurse. My dislike for this woman who was supposed to be interested in the best for patients was growing at a rapid speed. "So, give us a copy now, or I will call my attorney and have him come and take care of this."

"Humph, well, I can give your father a copy, but I certainly wouldn't give you one. Remember I don't even have to talk to you." She went over to her large copy machine and placed the document under the lid. When the copy spilled out, she brought it back over and gave it to Papa. "There you are sir. I hope this answers all your questions."

Papa looked at her and frowned, "No, it does not, and my daughter specializes in investigative work. She'll be checking into this, and if we have to get an attorney, we'll do so." Papa's face was red. I was worried about Papa's heart and that this whole scene was overtaxing his body.

It certainly looked like someone had added this statement after Papa signed it. Was this Andrea at work again with her conniving? She wanted to put Papa and Mama in the nursing home, and this would be the only way she could do it.

As we walked back toward Mama's room, Papa handed me the paper, "Patrice, hold on to this, we have to get this figured out. I'm telling you that statement was not on the paper I signed."

"I believe you, Papa. Don't worry; we'll check into this. Let's not tell Mama what's going on right now. She needs her rest."

"Good idea, Patrice. I don't want her upset." He stopped me in the hall right before we went back in Mama's room. "You know, your mother and I have always said we never wanted to go to a nursing home. We said we would take care of each other and that's what we'll do."

We spent the rest of the morning with Mama, in between visits from an occupational therapist, physical therapist, and speech therapist for evaluations. The doctor came in about 11:00. He asked Mama some questions and as he started to leave the room, I asked if Papa and I could talk to him in the hall.

The doctor led us to a small waiting area not far from Mama's room. We all sat down. Papa asked, "Doctor, tell us how bad this stroke is. My wife looks better this morning. Why are all these people coming in to evaluate her?"

"Your wife has had a stroke that has impacted part of her body. Currently she has no feeling on her left side and we are trying to determine the extent of her need for services when she leaves here."

Papa answered, "Patrice is my daughter, and she is going to help me get things organized when she comes home. We can take her to whatever therapies she needs."

"That's right. I'm Dr. Patrice Porter, and I have some time this summer to help my father with her care."

The doctor looked confused and said to my father, "Well, my office has already worked with Andrea Porter, and we are planning to get your wife moved to the Shady Oaks Nursing Home in a few days. You won't need to worry about her daily care."

Chapter Fifty-five

Summer, 1988

As Papa and I walked back to the room to be with Mama, we were very quiet. We knew we had to get this problem fixed. Andrea was not going to put Mama and Papa in that Shady place. "Don't worry, Papa, Jim is talking to his attorney, and he will help us out on this." I put my arm around Papa. I knew we had to get this mess straightened out and could not allow Andrea to engage in her manipulative behavior. I was more determined than ever that my parents were not going to a nursing home.

When we arrived back in the room, Mama was propped up in bed. "Well, what did the doctor say, James, about how I'm doing?" I knew Papa was going to have to lie because he wasn't going to say that Andrea wanted them in a nursing home. "The doctor said you're making progress. They have to work on your left arm and left leg."

"What's that mean, James? I'm worried. I don't feel my leg much. How come?"

I had been looking out the window as Papa answered her questions. I turned around and went over to Mama's bed. I straightened out Mama's covers. "You're going to get therapy to help you and once you get home, we'll take you to see the physical therapist and whoever else you need."

"But what if I can't walk? What will I do?"

"We'll help you. That's why the therapists were here to evaluate you."

We were saved from the continuation of this discussion when lunch arrived. Mama was busy eating when Andrew burst in, "Hi, Grandma, what's for lunch there?" Andrew went over and kissed Mama.

"Where's your dad?" Papa asked.

"Hi Grandpa. He's coming." He stopped and whispered in Papa's ear, "It's a surprise."

Jim walked in with a beautiful vase of flowers, "Hi, Annie. Thought you'd like a little cheer."

"Oh!" Mama cried. "You know how I love yellow flowers. They're beautiful. Just what I need to look at." Mama pushed her hair away from her face.

Jim sensed that we were not being overly talkative and must have something on our minds. I had gone back to the window and Papa was pacing the floor. "Hey, Patrice and James, how about I take you down to the cafeteria and get you some lunch. Andrew, will you stay here and keep your grandma company?"

"Sure, Dad. Hey Grandma, I even brought a deck of cards so we can play rummy."

"I don't know whether I can hold the cards, Andrew, but I'll try." Mama loved her only grandson and loved playing cards with him.

"It's okay, Grandma. I'll help you. Go on, Dad. You guys get some lunch."

As we went by the desk, I noticed the nasty nurse was gone. She must have either been taking a break or off duty. A cute blond nurse was there in her place, "Well hi, Jim, good to see you."

"Hey, Sandy, how are you? How's your son?"

"He's off to college, just like Andrew. Wants to study biology. Guess he takes after me liking science. He doesn't get it from his dad."

"Oh, pardon my manners, Sandy, this is my dear friend Patrice, Andrew's aunt and this is James, his grandpa." Jim looked at us.

"We're pleased to meet you, Sandy." I paused. "Who is that nurse who was here earlier today?"

"Oh, you mean the one with the red hair."

"Yes, that's the one." I answered.

"That's Betty. Why do you ask?"

"We just had difficulty getting some papers from her. She didn't want to give them to us but finally did."

Papa joined in the conversation, “Yes, I asked her for a copy of the papers that I had signed last night. She wouldn’t give them to Patrice. She finally gave them to me.”

“What kind of papers” Sandy asked.

“They were power of attorney papers. I have the copy of them.”

“Let me see them if you don’t mind.” Sandy asked.

“Sure, here they are.” I pulled the papers out of my purse.

Sandy frowned, “That’s funny. Let me check the records.” She walked away as Jim looked confused and said to me,” I guess I’m sorry I missed the exchange you must have had with, what did she say her name was, Betty?”

“Not the most pleasant person I’ve dealt with. I wanted to sock her.” I laughed now replaying the memory of the morning in my head. It hadn’t been funny at the time, that was for sure. I looked at Jim with his crisp tailored navy- blue suit and white shirt. I loved the tie he had on with it. Very light polka dots. Just like Jim to always make sure all his clothes matched. He played his role as an attorney and businessman well, and he had done well in his position as head of a large company that had been started by his father.

Sandy returned to where we were standing. "Sorry, that took me a few minutes, but look at this. Here's the document in the files and here's the copy of what you have." Jim and I looked at the papers she showed us. "The one in the file doesn't have anything about a power of attorney being Andrea Porter. That's been added on the one you were given."

Chapter Fifty-six

Summer, 1988

"It looks like my ex-wife is back to her games again, but this one is really bad. I'm so sorry, Patrice." Jim paused as we sat down to have our lunch in the cafeteria. We had gone through the line, and it was hard for me to pick out anything that looked good. I had lost my appetite but finally decided on a fish sandwich and a coffee. We just left our food dishes on the tray, more concerned about what we had just discovered.

"I can't believe it, Jim, she has done so much to mess up her own life but how could she do this to Mama and Papa, after all they've done for her." I took a sip of my coffee but decided it was still a bit too hot for me.

"What can we do? I know Andrea has always resented me, but how could she do this to her mother who has covered for her all her life?" Papa looked like he was going to cry. My heart was breaking for him, while at the same time I wanted to strangle my sister. Papa was right. Mama had done so much for her other daughter. She was the favorite one, and I never could do anything that pleased her.

I put my hand on Papa's arm. "We'll get this figured out. Don't worry."

"Okay, we have two issues here." Jim pulled his chair in as far as he could so no one else in the cafeteria could hear. He took my arm and Papa's arm. "First, Andrea has forged a document which is a very serious offense for which she can be prosecuted."

"Oh no, do we want to do that? I don't want to see her go to jail." I paused, "but at the same time, I don't want her to get away with this. What is the other issue?"

"That's the good part, Patrice, I met with my attorney friend who handles these kinds of cases, and he is drawing up the papers for James to be the power of attorney for finances and health for Annie, and if neither of you," he looked at James, "is able to make those decisions, Patrice will be power of attorney."

"Good, Jim, thank you for doing this. What do we need to do next? We have to act quickly so Andrea doesn't put me and Annie in that Sunny place nursing home." Papa asked.

Jim answered, "Well, I have arranged, if it's okay with both of you, to meet with the attorney to sign the papers in his office later today."

"Oh Jim, I can't thank you enough. You have been a godsend to us." I looked into Jim's eyes and a feeling like I had never had for this man came over me. I had the realization that he was the man I loved. Tears came to my eyes.

"Patrice, are you okay? Do you need to go home and rest?" Jim asked.

"Honey, if you want to rest, I'll stay here with your mother while you go take a nap at the house," Papa added.

"No, Papa, I'm okay." I straightened up to let Papa and Jim know that I was fine. I was trying to pull myself together. "Just give me a minute to use the ladies room and we'll go back and see Mama and Andrew." I smiled.

I found the closest restroom and went in and looked in the mirror. What was going on with me? I was mad at my sister, confused about what was happening with Mama, trying to protect Papa, and just had recognized that I loved a man who I had known for many years, yet had denied the feelings until today. I needed to pull myself together. I had to be strong. I took a Kleenex and wiped my face, stood up straight, and turned around and went back to the table, smiling at both Jim and Papa.

"Are you sure you're okay?" Papa asked.

"I'm fine. Let's go back and spend some time with Mama and then meet with the attorney and sign those papers."

Jim smiled, "Sounds like a plan to me."

When we got near Mama's room, we heard a loud cry from Mama. "No, I won't go. You can't make me." The nurse was coming from the opposite end, and we entered the room at the same time she did. "What's going on here, Mrs. Porter?" She looked at Andrea and Greg, who were in the room. Andrew looked at his father and blurted out. "They can't do this to Grandma, can they?"

The nurse asked Mama, "What has you so upset?" She looked at Andrea and Greg and said, "What did you say to her? We need to keep her quiet."

Andrew blurted out, "My mother says Grandma has to be moved to the nursing home this afternoon."

Chapter Fifty-seven

Summer, 1988

Jim replied to his son in a very firm voice, "Your grandma is not going to a nursing home, Andrew. As soon as she is cleared to leave, she is going home where your grandpa and Tice are going to take care of her and get her stronger."

I went over and patted Mama's hand and in a very calm voice said, "Don't worry, Mama, you aren't going anywhere but home."

Andrea spoke up, "The arrangements have already been made, thanks to Greg." She looked over and smiled at her boyfriend.

Jim spoke up, "Andrea, Greg, Patrice and I need to talk with you outside this room. James, do you want to stay here and keep Mama quiet, or do you want to come with us?"

"I know the two of you can clear this matter up. I'm going to stay here with Annie and Andrew." Papa went over and rubbed Mama's forehead and held a cup of water up to Mama's lips so she could take a sip.

When we got out in the hall, Andrea started talking. "Look, Greg has pulled a lot of strings to get my parents in the nursing home. It's all set. Case closed."

I spoke up as I stopped walking and looked my sister straight in the face. "There is no closed case. These are our parents, and I am not allowing you to put Mama and Papa in a nursing home."

Jim spoke up, "Patrice is right. Let's go to the visitors' room. Andrea, I don't think you want a commotion out here in the hall, but if you push it, we will consider having you arrested. Let's get down the hall before you and Greg are publicly embarrassed." He turned and looked at Greg with a disdainful look.

"Who do you think you are?" We were getting close to the nurse's station. "You are not even related to this family. You left my beautiful Andrea," Greg responded.

Jim stopped by the nurse's station. "Now you look here, buddy; I did not leave Andrea at all. I put up with her nonsense for a number of years. She was running around on me. She's all yours." Jim's face was turning red against the beautiful pale blue shirt he was wearing with his blue suit. "And another thing, the only thing that came out well in our relationship was Andrew, and your loving girlfriend couldn't even take care of him."

I commented, "Jim's right. And don't argue with us, just walk. You're in enough trouble."

When we arrived in the waiting area, the room was empty. I started by pulling the two papers out of my purse. "Andrea, you need to explain why one of these papers is different than the correct one in the files." I showed my sister the two pieces of paper, the one that said nothing about power of attorney and the other one that said Andrea Porter was power of attorney.

Andrea smirked, "I know nothing about that other sheet of paper, but this one clearly shows I am power of attorney, and that's why Mama and Papa are going to the nursing home."

Jim pointed to the one that said nothing about power of attorney and said, "Andrea, this is the correct paper that is in the file in the nurse's station, not this other document that appears to have been doctored by you or someone." He paused, "Do you want to explain this to us now or do you want us to press charges against you for presenting a fake document."

"You can't do this, Greg and I took care of this document, didn't we, Honey?"

"Of course, Darling, this is all finalized. These two need to get over it and accept the reality of the situation."

Jim leaned toward Greg, "We are on the way to sign legitimate papers that make James the power of attorney for Annie and, in the event that neither of them can make decisions, Patrice will be the power of attorney."

"That is so ridiculous, and you will not get away with this." Andrea stood up.

Jim stood up, once again with a red face. "Andrea and Greg, we can take this matter to the police if you want. It's your choice. Neither Patrice nor I are going to put up with your shenanigans anymore. What's it gonna be?"

Andrea took hold of Greg's arm, "Sweetie, let's get out of here. Obviously, we need to get an attorney. They want a fight; we'll give them one." On that note, they turned around and walked out of the visitors' room.

I turned to Jim, and he put his arms around me. His feelings of strength gave me courage. Papa and I were not alone in this fight with my sister. I looked Jim in the eyes and smiled, "Well, that went well."

"Does Andrea really think we are that stupid?" Jim said to me.

"She's about to find out we are not stupid at all. Let's go back to the room and get Papa and Andrew, and go get those papers signed," I answered.

"Wait, we had better leave Andrew here with Mama. I don't trust Andrea and Greg to come back and try something."

I answered, "You're right."

Jim and I walked back to Mama's room, quiet as we tried to digest all that had happened during the last twenty-four hours. We were looking down as we passed the nurse's station. "Oh, Jim," said the voice of the sweet nurse, Sandy, at the desk.

"Hi, Sandy, how's it going?"

"Are you going to see your friend Greg later today?" She asked. Friend was not a description I would use for Greg and Jim.

"No, I would say I won't see him." Jim answered. She seemed disappointed. "Why do you ask?"

"Oh darn, no I was supposed to give him a note from his sister today and I forgot. I was hoping you could deliver it for me."

"Sister? I didn't know Greg had a sister," I said confused.

"Oh yes, his sister works here at the desk as the charge nurse before I come on."

Chapter Fifty-eight

Summer, 1988

It had been two weeks since that fateful day when we discovered that Andrea and Greg had forged the document, with the help of Greg's sister who turned out to be the nasty nurse who worked the desk. When Jim and Papa and I had gone to the attorney to sign real papers so that Papa would be power of attorney, we had discussed options for legal actions. The forgery, of course was a crime but what did we want to do about it?

Papa had broken down and cried, "I can't believe my own daughter is a criminal. How could she do this to her own mother?" I relived that whole conversation one evening as I was still sleepless at 2 a.m.

The attorney had explained to us our options. We could press charges against all three of them, Greg, Greg's sister, and mine. I remembered his words, "You have to think long and hard about this. Do you want a messy trial, or do you want to just settle this?"

"Are those our only options? Is there anything else we can do?" Jim leaned forward as we sat in the attorney's office. This man was a well-respected attorney in town, as a matter of fact he was a partner with Jesse, Andrea's first husband.

I spoke up as I braced myself in the chair where I sat. "I don't want to send my sister to jail. Mama would never approve, even after Andrea tried to put her away." I paused. "I sure don't care though about Greg and that horrible sister of his. They are scum."

The attorney stood up and moved away from his chair and sat on the edge of the desk. He put his hand to his chin. "Here is the other option that I am recommending, and I want you to think about it."

Jim put his hand on mine, "Sure, tell us and we'll discuss it."

The attorney continued, "I can go to the hospital administrator and show him what Greg's sister did and tell him we will settle out of court if she is fired immediately. Otherwise, we will file charges against her and go public with what the hospital allowed to happen." He stood up and went over to his window which overlooked a peaceful garden area. "Think about it tonight and let me know in the morning."

I stood up, "We will, and Jim will get back to you in the morning." I looked at my Papa. He looked like he had aged ten years. I took him by the hand. "Come on, Papa. It'll all work out."

On the way home that day, we all agreed that this was the best plan. I remembered saying, "I just hate it, though, that Greg gets off scot free."

Jim had answered, "I know but somehow I think he would never go down by himself, and do we want Andrea going down with him?"

"You're right." I turned and looked at Papa in the back seat and knew we were doing the right thing.

Tonight, we were sitting at the dinner table at our house, Jim, me, Andrew, and my parents. Mama had insisted on trying to cook. She was home from the hospital and getting stronger every day but the feeling in her left arm and leg had not returned. She was in therapy, but we had been told the feeling might not come back. I knew she couldn't cook alone so I had helped her. I could see the frustration on her face, but she tried to do as much with her right hand as possible. We finally sat down to the meatloaf dinner.

"Darn," Papa said.

"What's the matter?" I asked right after we all sat down.

"I forgot to take my heart medicine." Papa seemed so tired he just couldn't get up.

"No worry, Grandpa, I'll get it." Andrew said.

"Andrew, it's okay, tell Mama and Papa about your college roommate you met yesterday. I'll get the pills." I got up and went to the cabinet in the kitchen where Papa kept his pills right beside Mama's medicine.

I looked at the medicine bottle to make sure it was my father's medicine. It was the right one. I happened to look at the dosage. I had never really looked closely at the prescription. Papa was capable of taking his pills himself. Papa was to take two pills each evening with his dinner.

I opened the bottle to take the two pills out, not wanting to take the whole container to the dinner table. I picked up the pills and I looked at the dosage on one of the pills. I looked at the container again. Each pill was double the milligrams that the prescription on the label said.

Chapter Fifty-nine

Summer, 1988

"How come Andrea hasn't come by?" Mama asked me one afternoon when I was helping her put the wash away.

"I don't know." I knew why but wasn't going to upset my mother, so I changed the subject. "Mama, Cecilia is in town and is coming over to see us."

"Should I make dinner for her?"

"Oh no, Mama, that is too much for you. She is coming over later to see us, but maybe we can make a dessert to serve." My mother was still having trouble fixing dinner and I needed to help her so we could put together a dessert for later. "What would you like to have?"

"How about a lemon meringue pie?"

"That sounds yummy, but you will have to do a lot of it because I have too much trouble making meringue." I paused. Mama looked tired. "Why don't you go sit and watch TV with Papa and I'll finish this. I need to make a phone call anyway."

I thought back to the night before last. When I had noticed the discrepancy with Papa's medication, I had only given Papa one of the pills. Then later Jim and I had gone to my room and made a phone call to my friend, Cecilia, who was the cardiologist. I told her that I had noticed that the dosage on the pills was different than what was on the bottle. Cecilia had told me to continue to just give one of the pills to Papa.

Then what a relief I felt when she said, "Patrice, you are going through too much alone. I have a few days off coming up day after tomorrow. I'm going to fly out and help you and Jim get to the bottom of this."

"Oh Cecilia, I can't impose on you like that." Jim and I were sitting on my bed side by side in the room that used to be Andrea's. Jim had his arm around me. I leaned my head into his chest. Cecilia's response had been, "Patrice, that's what friends are for you need help and I'm going to give it to you." We hung up and I told Jim what Cecilia had said.

Memories of that night had come back. Was this a mistake of the pharmacy or was it the doctor's mistake? It was someone's and we were going to get to the bottom of it. My dear friend would help us.

I had heard from Cecilia when she arrived at our Holiday Inn where she was staying. She would be over at seven. We had finished our dinner. "Mama, you sit and rest now. Jim and I are going to go over to the hotel and pick Cecilia up."

When we pulled up to the lobby door, Cecilia was there waiting outside on a bench. She looked as beautiful with her long dark hair and her slim body. I felt such a sense of relief that she was here, and she would help us sort this out. I got out of the car and gave her a big hug. "I'm so glad you're here." Jim got out of the car and I smiled, "Cecilia, you remember Jim?"

Cecilia gave him an approving look, "I'm so happy to get to see you again, although I wish this situation wasn't happening to your family."

Jim smiled at her, "You don't know how good it is to see you. I can't begin to tell you how much I appreciate you coming to help us."

"Well, let's get started," Cecilia said as she moved toward the car. Jim opened the back door for her. When we were situated in the car, she added "Okay, tell me what's going on. I know Andrea pulled one of her stunts, and it was bad." I had called her about the situation with the forged papers. "You both were a lot nicer to her than I would have ever been, but I understand you were trying to keep peace."

"Exactly," Jim said as we sat in the car before pulling out. "The administrator did fire Greg's sister and we talked to Andrea and Greg and let them know that what they did was criminal."

I added as I turned to look at Cecilia in the back seat. "Cecilia, it was awful, Andrea called both of us names and said how dare we accuse her and Greg of doing such a thing. We remained calm and told her if they ever did anything like that again, we would press charges. We then told them that we were not telling Mama about this."

"That was a wise decision. In your mother's condition, she does not need any stress." Cecilia leaned forward. "But has Andrea told her mother her side of the story?"

Jim turned around. "Andrea has not seen her mother since. We don't know what she is up to. Hey, let's go get some of that lemon pie that Patrice and her mother made, and you can look at the pills." Jim pulled out of the lobby parking area.

When we arrived, we found Mama and Papa sitting in the living area, both dozing.

"Look who's here." Jim said.

They both woke up with a start and then realized Cecilia was in the room. Papa got up and hugged Cecilia. Mama stayed in her chair, still trying to wake up.

"You all chat and I will serve the pie." I said as I moved toward the kitchen. I cut the pieces of pie and Mama had the decaf coffee in the percolator. I came out from the kitchen, and said, "goodies are served." Everyone came to the table, and we enjoyed the time together. "This pie is fabulous" Jim commented as he put another big bite in his mouth.

Cecilia then got to the point, "James do you care if I come over in the morning and examine you? I want to see what's going on and why you're so tired."

"Sure, can't beat having the best cardiologist in the country see me."

Cecilia blushed, "Tell me a little bit more about how you've been feeling."

"I've just been so tired. I thought the heart pills would make me feel better. I guess they are supposed to slow me down, but those pills are overdoing it. Patrice told me you said to cut the pills back to see if I felt better."

"Let me see your pill bottle." Cecilia said. "Did you take them tonight?" I got up and retrieved the pill bottle.

"I took just one instead of two."

"Well, let me take these pills with me and see what I can find out."

"Can we get you anything else?" I asked.

"No, speaking of being tired, I'm that and just need to get back to the hotel and get a good night's rest." She paused, "Just one more question, James."

"Sure, anything," Papa answered.

"Did you pick this prescription up yourself? I just wondered who filled it at the drug store when you picked it up." Cecilia was looking at the pill bottle and opened it up to see the pills in it.

"I didn't pick it up. Greg personally delivered it himself the last time."

Chapter Sixty

Summer, 1988

I met Cecilia for a late breakfast the next morning. I had suggested that we have breakfast at the hotel before I took her back over to the house so she could examine Papa. She was already seated in the dining room in one of the booths when I arrived. I smiled. How wonderful it was she was here to figure out what might be happening to my father. She stood up and we hugged. "Did you get a good night's sleep?" I asked her as I took a whiff of the coffee smell, mixed with bacon, aroma that permeated the room.

"I sure did and decided I am treating myself to a real breakfast this morning." She paused, "I usually just have an apple and coffee."

I laughed, "Same here when I'm back in my condo, but Mama treats me while I'm home. She wants to cook but it's tough for her."

"How's she done with the emotional trauma from her stroke?" Cecilia leaned forward as she closed her menu.

"It's frustrating for her because she doesn't have much feeling in her left arm and leg, but she doesn't complain much." I took a sip of my coffee. "What's tough for her is that Andrea doesn't have anything to do with her. You know, I joke with Jim that Andrea has become her fair-weather daughter."

"What do you mean?" Cecilia asked.

"Well, you know, here's my theory. Andrea has obsessive compulsive disorder, and she likes everything perfect. Her mama is no longer that way, and I think Mama disgusts Andrea. She isn't perfect in her eyes anymore, so she wants nothing to do with her."

"That makes sense," Cecilia looked pensive. "I never thought that a person with obsessive compulsive disorder would shut out the person who doted on her, but I guess that makes sense."

"Let me tell you though, I'm glad she's not around. I don't have to worry about her saying nasty stuff about me to Mama." I stopped. "Isn't it funny, the least favorite daughter, me, is the one taking care of her mother, while the preferred daughter has jumped ship when her mother isn't perfect anymore."

We were interrupted by the waitress who came to take our order. We treated ourselves to two eggs, pancakes, and grits. We caught up on Cecilia's career and her love life. I suspected a marriage proposal from her significant other before long.

Cecilia leaned forward and whispered, "Tell me about Jim. What's happening? You know that guy is so in love with you. You make the perfect couple."

"The perfect couple with my sister right in the middle. This just can never be. Andrea will always stand in our way." I said as I took a sip of my water.

"Only if you let her, Patrice. I just don't want to see you let Andrea prevent your happiness. She's not worth it." She stopped. "By the way, is that sleazy Greg she's living with as OCD as she is?"

I laughed at Cecilia's statement. Our food arrived. "Ooh, this is yummy! Gosh Cecilia, I miss you. Yes, Greg is as ridiculous as she is. Andrew says when he goes over there, he's not allowed to wear shoes in the house and all the furniture is covered with plastic. Heaven forbid anything gets dirty."

We finished breakfast, I paid the bill, and we headed over to the house so she could look at Papa. After she had examined him and asked him a few questions, she asked Papa to sign a release to talk to his doctor. She then went over to the phone and made a call to Papa's doctor. She asked if we could stop by his office this afternoon.

I asked Andrew if he could come over and spend some time with Mama. I just wasn't comfortable leaving her alone. Cecilia, Papa, and I went to the doctor's office around four that afternoon. The waiting room was empty by that time, and the office nurse escorted us into Doctor

Peterson's office. The doc had been Papa's GP for years. He gave Papa a confused look, "James, you don't look so good. What's the matter?" Papa explained that he was just so tired, some days he could barely get out of bed.

Cecilia pulled the pill bottle out of her purse. "Doctor Peterson, this is the prescription for James, and we are trying to find an explanation. We were hoping you could help. The dosage on the bottle does not match the pills in the container."

Doctor Peterson reached over to look at the pills. He read the label and then looked at the pills.

"You can see why we wanted to talk with you today. The pills say one thing and the medicine dosage you prescribed says another. This can explain why James is so tired. He's taking too high of a dosage." Cecilia said.

"Wait a minute, I never prescribed this medication at all for James. This is the wrong medicine and the wrong dosage."

Chapter Sixty-One

Summer, 1993

"I certainly hope you're satisfied, Miss Big Shot. Look at what you've done." Andrea scowled at me and Jim as we came out of the courtroom. We felt a sense of relief that this long and drawn-out investigation was now over. Greg would serve five years in prison for what he had done. My sister Andrea was put on probation.

I frowned at her, "Andrea, you did all of this to yourself. You made the choice to get involved with Greg and to put your own father's life at risk to make sure your boyfriend made a buck." I paused as I felt my face getting red at the memories of what Andrea had done to Papa.

Jim was standing beside me, and we started to walk away.

"Oh yes, the happy little couple." Andrea glared at me. "You took my husband away from me and then tried to frame me and my Greg. Well, let me tell you one thing, little sister, you've not heard the last from me. I'll get you before this is all over."

Jim stood in between my sister and me speaking in a very stern voice, "Andrea, that sounds like a threat. You're on probation. Either you get going and we never see your ugly face again or I will notify your probation officer. Understand, don't come near my fiancé ever again and don't go crying to my son."

Andrea pulled out a Kleenex to dab her eyes, faking tears. She looked at Jim, "You're despicable. What did I ever see in you?" She walked away.

Jim gave me a hug, "Are you okay?" I pulled away and looked into his eyes. "Yes, I'm fine and so relieved justice was gotten for Greg."

"Hey, it's been a long day. Let's go celebrate our engagement."

"You didn't forget my promise, did you?" I had promised Jim that, once this trial was over, we would become engaged. I smiled at the thought. "Can we stop by the house and tell Papa?"

Mama and Papa were still living in their home. Since Papa's medication was changed that fateful day when we started unraveling the pieces of the web that Greg and Andrea had weaved, he was doing great and was able to take care of Mama. All of the events that had become public about Andrea's role in Greg's scheme had been difficult for her. We tried to keep many of the details from her. She still defended her daughter and never believed that her beautiful daughter would do anything to harm her. We refrained from any arguments with her and tried not to say much about the particulars that had come out in the trial.

When we pulled in the driveway, Papa saw us pull in and came out on the porch. "What happened? Was it just another day with no decision made?"

I hugged Papa, "It's over. Greg was sentenced today to five years in the Crawfordsville prison."

My father pulled away and looked at me with that worry that had captured his face throughout the trial. "What will Andrea do now? She's maintained his innocence through this whole thing. It's the only way she's saved face."

"I don't know, Papa. She's very angry at me and blames me."

"That's my daughter. Never taking responsibility for anything she does. Patrice, what would I do without you? I feel like so much of this is my fault. If only I would have made her stay in counseling all those years ago, this may not have happened."

Jim looked at my father with an understanding look, "James, there was nothing you could have done for Andrea. She would never have accepted help." He paused and looked down, "I should have made her get help when she wasn't taking care of my son. I knew she was disturbed, and I did nothing."

"Wait a minute, you two." I interrupted both of them. "Andrea has been very disturbed for a long time, as a matter of fact, I knew it when she beat me that night." I stopped and looked at both of them, "The important point here is that we can no longer allow Andrea to control our life. I, for one, from this day forward will not allow her to do so and it starts with some good news, Papa."

"Tell me, Patrice, I need good news."

I smiled, "You are going to have a son-in-law back." I took Jim's hand. "I promised Jim that when this trial was finished, I would marry him and that is what I intend to do."

Mama must have heard us out on the porch, and she came out the door. "What did I hear about marriage?" I repeated what I had said. Jim smiled as I gave him a kiss on the cheek.

"That's okay, I guess, but I just got some good news."

"What's that, Mama? I looked confused.

"Andrea is moving back home with us."

Chapter Sixty-two

Summer, 1993

We had been shocked when Mama broke the news that Andrea planned to move back home and were even more shocked when Papa had looked her right in the eye and said, “Annie, Andrea is not welcome in our home. She has a home she can live in or she can move into an apartment. She won’t be under this roof.”

“James, how can you say that? She’s our daughter and she needs us. She can help me around the house.”

I couldn’t keep quiet. We were still standing out on the front porch, “Mama has Andrea helped you for the last five years?”

“That’s different,” sniffled Mama. “You and James wouldn’t give her a chance. You blamed her for everything that boyfriend of hers did. It wasn’t Andrea’s fault.”

Jim interrupted. He saw that the conversation was going nowhere. “Hey, we can discuss this later. Patrice and I have an errand to run and then we’re going out to dinner to celebrate.”

“Celebrate? We have nothing to be excited about. My poor Andrea needs me and you’re going out?”

Papa took my mother by the arm, “Yes, Annie, they’re going out. Let’s go inside and start dinner.” He took Mama by the arm. She still had a slight limp from her stroke, but it had gotten better after a number of sessions of physical therapy that she had since the time of her stroke.

Jim and I walked to the car saying nothing. When we got in the car, he announced, “I don’t know about you, but I am so angry at Andrea’s latest trick, we’re going to take care of it.”

“Are you thinking what I’m thinking? We’re going to pay a visit to her probation officer?”

“Scary, how we think alike now, isn’t it?” Jim looked over at me and smiled. “We’ve been through a lot together and I can’t wait for more, but first, let’s pay a visit to probation.”

“Why would Andrea want to move back in our house? She lives in that beautiful home that Greg’s parents gave them when they moved in together.” I looked over at Jim as he maneuvered the streets on our way to the downtown courthouse where the probation department was.

“Patrice, Greg’s parents may have money with all those nursing homes they run but think of all the legal fees they have paid for attorneys for their son.”

"You're right. They must have paid the whole bill so he would keep his mouth shut and not implicate them. They had to have known about his scheme to drug people so they would become so debilitated that he could tell the family about the nursing home that his parents had listed him and his sister as owners."

"It was quite a scheme Greg and, unfortunately your sister and my ex-wife were part of it. None of it would have ever been discovered if Andrea and her boyfriend would not have tried to drug your father." Jim pulled up to a stoplight and looked over at me.

"Well, luckily Greg won't be doing that anymore and hopefully the thirty people that were sitting in that horrible nursing home are doing better and some have been able to go home." I commented as Greg pulled in the parking lot behind the courthouse.

"Well, let's see what we need to do next. I'm so proud of your dad telling Annie that Andrea couldn't move back in." Jim said as he came around and opened the door for me.

Because Jim was a prominent member in the community because of the business he ran and his family was also well known and influential in the community, he only had to go to the receptionist for the probation office and say he wanted to see Mr. Ransom and the receptionist was polite and said, "Just a minute, I'm sure Mr. Ransom will see you."

Andrea's probation officer came out, looking a bit tired and disheveled like it had been a rough day, and he motioned for us as he said, "Come on back."

He offered us a seat in his messy office where papers were strewn all over. I was thinking that this office where Andrea was going to have to report would drive her up a wall with her obsessive-compulsive behaviors.

"What can I do for the two of you?" her probation officer said as he went around to his desk chair.

"This deals with Andrea Porter's living situation that you must have agreed to," Jim said as he leaned forward.

Ransom frowned, "Just what living situation did I agree to?"

It was my turn to lean forward, and I said, "That my sister could move back in with our parents. Let me tell you, Mr. Ransom, that is not acceptable. Andrea, together with her boyfriend who was just sentenced today, overdosed my father. There is no way I'm letting her in that house and, speaking for my father, he also says no." My voice had gone up at least two notches.

"Would you prefer your sister to be homeless? She has no money and nowhere to live."

"She has that beautiful home that Greg's parents gave them when Greg and Andrea moved in together."

Jim added, "And I still give her sizeable alimony as part of our divorce settlement when she was supposed to be raising my son. I'm afraid I never went back to court to fight her to stop it. My son is now out on his own and she hasn't had him in her care for years, especially after she was leaving him unsupervised."

"Hold it! I'm afraid I'm a bit lost here." Mr. Ransom went over and opened up his four-drawer old gray file cabinet that was banged up. He took out a file from his top drawer.

"I wouldn't ordinarily be able to give you this information but since you're telling me your money is involved, I need to let you know something." He came back to his desk and sat back down. "According to the information, I have, Andrea had a written agreement with Greg's parents."

"What kind of written agreement are you talking about?" I asked as I held my purse closer to my chest.

"Well, every month, Andrea was supposed to give money, I guess that was the money you gave her, to Greg's parents as part of the payment on the house. Now, it seems that the parents want her to move out right away."

"That shouldn't be a problem. She can afford a little apartment with the money I still give her monthly. I won't stop doing that as long as she causes no trouble for us, that includes not moving back in with the Porter's." My fiancé answered.

"Jim, there's a big problem here."

"What is it? Seems simple to me; guess I will be paying her rent from now on." Jim looked over at me and shook his head like he couldn't believe we were going to be taking care of Andrea.

"The problem is," Mr. Ransom paused as he looked at me. "Andrea has not been paying them the money they are due for the last four years. She owes them a lot of money and they want it and want it right now."

Chapter Sixty-three

Summer, 1993

"Patrice, I need to let you know how much I was paying Andrea in alimony. You have to be wondering and now this is going to impact you directly." Jim leaned toward me as we were seated at the Italian restaurant just north of the city that was one of our favorite places to be. "I don't want any secrets in our marriage."

I took a sip of my Moscato and answered Jim. "It was really none of my business before. I thought it had to be quite a bit of money. What I don't understand is why were Greg's parents charging Andrea. They are very wealthy." I paused. "Unfortunately, at the expense of the elderly in their despicable nursing homes."

"You're so right. They are as treacherous as their son. They had to have known that their son was feeding them business by drugging people." Jim closed his menu. "Unless, they had something on Andrea and were blackmailing her."

"Jim, you've been around me and your son doing investigative reporting too long. I think you are on to something, and it's time we had a talk with my sister to find out what's going on."

"My thought, exactly. I really don't want to think that Andrea was involved in this scam, but she may have been." Jim paused. "I know my ex-wife and how she loves the finer things in life and there's something we're missing."

"I agree, Andrea was probably buying a wardrobe full of expensive clothes, at your expense," I said.

"First things first, Andrea is moving into a small efficiency apartment and she's going to get a job to pay back the money she owes Greg's parents." Jim put his hand on mine.

I had to laugh, "Oh, that's not going to go over well at all. Andrea in an efficiency apartment and not everything she wants. I can't even fathom that."

"We're going to develop the plan for her to continue to get the $2,000 a month in alimony I'm giving her. I control the purse strings, so to speak, and she won't have any say."

"So, you'll pay for the efficiency apartment directly to the landlord and the remainder of the money will go to Greg's parents?" I clarified and was thinking how Andrea had been on the gravy train for a long time and the party was about to be over.

"I think we better be doing some negotiating and seeing why Greg's family wanted money from Andrea. They are quite wealthy, and a number of people have not trusted them for a long time. This sounds fishy to me," Jim added.

Our food had arrived. The aroma of sauces and garlic was yummy. "Ooh, this looks great," I said. After the waiter put the food on the table, I said, "And no doubt it is fishy. I think another meeting with the probation officer and Andrea is in order."

"Do you want me to set it up?" Jim asked as he looked down at his plate in preparation for his first bite.

"For sure, I am fine tomorrow. I'm doing some work on my fall syllabi to get ready for classes, but I can take a break anytime."

We finished our lovely dinner. By then it was about ten p.m. Andrew was sitting on the porch as we pulled in Mama and Papa's and got out of the car. He had a big smile on his face. "Grandma and Grandpa are already in bed. Did you have a good time? When's the wedding?"

Andrew was eager for us to set the wedding. He was out of school and now had a position at the newspaper where I had been editor. He was dating a beautiful young lady who was a teacher in the same town as the newspaper. He and I were planning a book that would be an expose on practices in nursing homes and had completed a great deal of the research already.

He was sad about his mother, but before he had gone off to college, he had accepted the fact that his mother had serious mental illness. He no longer wanted to see us suffer at her expense. He and I had long talks about his viewpoints about his mother.

Jim asked his son a question, "Did your mother call here tonight?"

"Yes, she said she was staying in a hotel and the probation officer told her she couldn't live here. She said you were being mean to her." Andrew answered, "I can't wait to hear the real story."

"We told her that was not acceptable at all that she live here. I will keep giving her money to get an efficiency apartment." Jim answered.

"Uh, I need to tell you that there was another call," Andrew said.

"Who from?" I asked, worried about the answer I might get.

"Grandpa took the call. It seems it was Greg's father, and it upset Grandpa."

"Did he say what it was about?" Jim asked.

"Yes, he was upset because Mr. Osbourn, Greg's father, said that Andrea owes them money and if Andrea doesn't pay, they will take this house away from them."

Chapter Sixty-four

Summer, 1993

I was helping Mama put some clothes away after she had done the wash. I enjoyed getting to spend some time with her and was glad she had made improvements after her stroke. She still had no feeling in her left arm, but she worked hard to cover that up. Mama asked, "I don't understand why Andrea can't live here anymore? James just doesn't understand her. It would be like old times to have her back here with us."

I wanted to argue but knew that was futile. Mama still couldn't understand that Andrea only wanted to live at home because she was out of money and had nowhere else to go. "Mama, Andrea's boyfriend tried to hurt Papa, and Andrea probably knew it. She can't stay here." I spoke in a calm but firm voice.

The phone rang. I answered it because I knew that it was probably Jim. "Sure, two-thirty works fine. I'll be there." I went out to the yard and told Papa that Jim and I were meeting with the probation officer and Andrea was going to be there.

"What's going to happen to Andrea now? Am I going to lose our house?" Papa's face showed more wrinkles. I knew he had probably had a sleepless night.

"No, Papa, you are not going to lose this house. Jim and I'll do everything possible to keep that from happening." I gave him a hug. "Don't worry. Wish us luck with the probation officer. Andrea's not gonna be happy."

Jim had told me to meet him outside the courthouse because he didn't want either of us to have to face Andrea alone if she was waiting for the meeting.

Jim gave me a peck on the cheek when I walked toward him. He commented, "Well, let's see what we can get done."

"I'm sure not looking forward to this." I commented as I looked him in the eye with an admiring stare, "but we'll get through it together."

We arrived a little before 2:30 and were expecting to see Andrea already in the waiting area outside the probation officer's room.

When Mr. Ransom saw us, he motioned for us to come on in. He looked at me, "Do you know where your sister is? I told her she had to be here at 2:30. I guess she's got another minute or two." He looked at his watch.

While we were waiting, Jim explained what Andrea had attempted the night before, asking if she could move in with her mother and father. He also shared the information about Greg's father calling and threatening that he would take the house away from Papa if Andrea's bills weren't paid.

"Wait a minute. You've lost me. You told me that you were giving Andrea $2,000 a month. Why wasn't Andrea able to pay them the money they wanted?"

"Good question," I said, "that's what I hope we can find out today from my sister." It was now 2:40 and no sign of Andrea. Mr. Ransom was looking at his watch. He picked up his phone and dialed it, trying to reach her. He hung up. "No answer. If she isn't here in the next ten minutes, I can have the police go find her. She's on probation and has to see me when I say so."

"Oh no, what can she be thinking?" I shook my head.

In walked Andrea, upset but putting on her usual arrogant face. "What are these two doing here?" She scowled as she looked at us. I knew that ugly look of hers well from all the years I had to deal with her. Her ugliness had always been masked by her physically beautiful face.

"The critical question here is where have you been? You came this close to being arrested." Mr. Ransom put up two of his chubby fingers close together.

"Arrested? Why would you do that?" Andrea got a puzzled look on her face.

"Because when I tell you to be in my office at two-thirty, I want you in my office at two-thirty. Understand?

So, give me a reason why you weren't here on time and give me a reason why you owe your boyfriend's family so much money." He paused and looked down at a file. "Your ex-husband has told me he gives you two thousand dollars a month so why haven't you been paying the so-called rent, to Greg's parents. That's a lot of money."

"I have good reason I wasn't here, but I sure don't want to disclose my personal life to these two." She looked down at us and frowned. She was still standing.

"I don't really care at this point, Miss Porter, you'll give us your excuse or I'll let you sit in jail for twenty-four hours. What's it gonna be?" He paused. "Sit down and start talking or I'll get the bailiff here to escort you away to your new home?"

"Well, this certainly doesn't have anything to do with these two." Andrea scowled at us.

"I believe it does. You've been getting money from Jim every month and now we find out you owe money to Greg's parents and they're threatening to take your parents' house away." Her probation officer raised his voice.

I paused and was getting angrier at Andrea's latest scam. "So, for the record, it is very much our business."

"First things first," Mr. Ransom said as he rocked back in his chair that needed to be oiled. "Why weren't you here in time?"

"I can explain." Andrea said.

"By all means do right now, as a matter of fact." The probation officer said as he took a drink of a cup of coffee. "You're wasting a lot of our time."

Andrea said in a quiet voice, "I'm being blackmailed."

Chapter Sixty-five

Summer, 1994

I had been amazed at the mess that my sister had gotten herself into. It had now been a year since we learned that she was being blackmailed by Greg's parents. Of course, they denied it and Andrea had no proof. The probation officer suspected that she had been spending the money she was supposed to pay them for "rent" on clothes. That was possible knowing my sister's love of beautiful and expensive clothes, but I couldn't help but wonder whether there was more to the story.

After a talk with the attorney we had hired, Greg's parents backed away from charging Andrea any money that she was reported to owe them. That was suspicious. They also had backed away from their threats to take Mama and Papa's home away.

Andrew was doing well in his job at the newspaper, and we continued to work on our book to expose some of the corruption in nursing homes. Jim and I had gotten married over the Christmas holiday, and I felt happier than I had ever been before. It was a very small affair with just Mama and Papa and Andrew. We were in the process of building our own home in the town where I had grown up and where Jim continued to live.

Since I didn't have to go into the university every day, I didn't mind commuting the hour each way.

I will never forget the look on Andrea's face at the probation office, when she was told that she would have to go to work and get an efficiency apartment. Jim had been very firm when he said, "I will no longer support you, Andrea, you got yourself in this mess and I have been paying you money for years, and no more." Andrea had left town and found an efficiency apartment close to the prison where Greg was housed. She had never had a job in her life and was working at a secretary in an office.

I wasn't teaching this summer so was enjoying the time with Jim. We were outside looking at our dream home which was half built now when Andrew stopped by. We loved to come over late in the afternoon and look at the progress that was being made on a home that would be totally ours. "Hey, buddy, how's it going?" Jim asked as I gave this wonderful young man a hug.

"Tice, have you got some time tomorrow to meet with me on the book? I have an interesting twist in this story."

"Sure, do you want me to come into the newspaper or do you want to meet at the house?" I answered. "Either is fine with me."

"I've got some files I want to show you at the office, if you don't mind."

"No problem. I'll be there around ten."

"Andrew, is something bothering you?" Jim asked his son.

"Kind of. Can I take you two to dinner and we can talk about it?" Andrew asked trying to smile but having to make a real effort.

"Hey, it is dinner time. Let's do it." Jim answered.

We ended up at our favorite Italian restaurant. "I'm hungry for fettucine alfredo." I said as we looked at the menus. I felt such contentment. Here I was with my husband and nephew.

"Sounds good to me too. How about you, Andrew?"

"I'm not real hungry, guys. I might just have the fried cheese appetizer."

As soon as we ordered, Jim asked his son, "Okay, what's up, Andrew? Something's going on. Is it a story you're writing?"

Andrew took a drink of the beer he had ordered, "No, Dad. It's about my mom."

"What's she done now?" Jim asked with a scowl on his face, taking the words right out of my mouth.

Andrew frowned, "Well, I got a call from some guy named Marcus who knows Mom."

I took a sip of my Moscato, "Has she got a new boyfriend?"

"I don't think it's a new boyfriend. Do you remember her ever mentioning someone by that name? It sounds familiar, but I can't figure out why."

"Marcus, that doesn't ring a bell for me. Does it you, Patrice?" Jim asked.

I leaned toward Andrew. "What did the guy say?" I had been enjoying the aroma of the Italian spices in the restaurant until now. My curiosity took control.

"That's the problem. He asked me where she was living." Andrew took a big drink of his beer. "When I wouldn't tell him and asked him why he wanted to know, he yelled, "Just tell her I better get what she owes me, and it better be soon."

Chapter Sixty-six

Summer, 1994

During my hour drive to meet Andrew at his office, my old stomping ground, I was thinking about our conversation at dinner and kept going over in my head who was Marcus. Was it a previous boyfriend that Andrea had? The name just didn't ring a bell for me.

As I pulled into a visitor spot at the newspaper office where I had been the editor for several years, I thought about how lucky I was to have gotten such good experience there. I missed being in the newspaper business but remembered the long hours. I was single back then and was wedded to my work. Now, with my marriage to Jim, I was wedded to my husband and realized he came first for me. I had waited so long to have a life with the man I loved that he would be my priority.

Even though Andrew and I were busy working on our new book to expose the nursing home business, I put Jim first, and Andrew and I involved Jim in some of our research on the book, so it was a family affair. I had tenure at the university now so I could choose my schedule of classes and only had them three days a week. That allowed more writing time and more focus on my husband.

When I walked into the newspaper office, I was greeted by many familiar faces. There were folks who had devoted their entire career to the paper, and there were new people who I had met through Andrew's work there. Andrew was now assistant editor, and I knew it was only a matter of time before he would be promoted. I wasn't prejudiced at all. I knew a talented newsman when I saw one.

Andrew greeted me as I walked in and gave me a big hug. He looked like he was eager to tell me something. As he escorted me into his small office, he said, "Hey Tice, let me get you some coffee."

"No need to do that, I can get it myself. The coffee pot hasn't moved. Do you need a refill?" I looked in his coffee cup and saw it was almost empty. "Let me get yours. I guess I know where the famous Bunn-o-Matic is." I swear it was the same electric coffee maker they had when I was there. It hadn't been replaced.

As I carried the two coffees back into his office, Andrew said as he went over to the door, "Let's close this. I've got something to share that we need to discuss privately before we get to work on our book."

"What's up, Andrew? Is it something about the book or about our conversation last night about the guy named Marcus?"

Andrew was seated at his desk and was tapping his pen. "Tice, I finally figured out who Marcus is, and I've started unraveling this mystery."

I leaned forward in my chair, "You've got my attention. What's up?"

Late last night when I couldn't sleep, I kept going over who Marcus could be. It finally dawned on me that a couple of years ago when I had dinner with Mom, she said she had an agent.

"An agent? What on earth would she have an agent for? Did she mean a real estate agent?" I thought maybe she was moving out of Greg's house and needed to find someone to locate a new home for her.

Andrew laughed, "Not quite." My mother said she had been approached by an agent who was so stricken with her beauty that he wanted her to become a model."

"Oh no, that's the oldest line in the book. Let me guess this guy's name was Marcus and she was paying him to get her modeling." I rolled my eyes because this sounded just like something Andrea would do. She was always so vain and not too smart.

"Tice, this gets worse. I called Mother this morning to tell her about the phone call I got. She didn't want to tell me." Andrew stood up and came around the desk and sat on his desk facing me. "She started crying and said he never got her a modeling job. I kept pressing her for his last name. At first, she clammed up. I tried to tell her that no one could protect her from this guy if she didn't tell me who it was. Anyway, she finally spilled it out."

"Do I want to know more about this mess Andrea is in? Her situation just keeps getting worse and frankly I am worried for you. This guy knows who you are and that you are her son."

"Yes, I'm afraid he does know who I am. Mother told him she had a son and he tracked me down."

"I figure you have already checked this guy out. Let me guess he's not an agent for reputable models." I leaned back in my chair and put my head back to look up at the ceiling.

"You've got it." Andrew paused and in a quiet voice said, "Oh Tice, he's involved in porn films."

Chapter Sixty-seven

Summer, 1994

My mouth dropped open at Andrew's news about his mother and my sister Andrea. Never in my wildest dreams would I have suspected that she would get herself involved in pornography. I hated to ask this about my nephew's mother but felt I had to, "Has she been in any porn films?"

"Oh, Tice, I don't know. I pray that she hasn't been, but we have to find out."

"Okay, Andrew, let's think. If she is a victim of blackmail, we need to let her probation officer know. We also need to tell your father what we know, and we need to talk to Andrea, whether she wants to talk or not." I paused, "Why don't you call your mother at work and tell her we need to talk with her as soon as she gets off? We can meet her at her apartment. I'll then call your father and let him know and see what he wants to do about notifying her probation officer." I put my hand on Andrew's arm feeling so bad for him, and realizing that, besides finding out such an awful thing about his mother, he was in danger because of what his mother did.

"Thanks, Tice, for giving us a plan. I have been sick over this since she told me last night." Andrew stood up and went back around to his desk and picked up the phone. “Mom, we need to see you tonight. We’ll meet you at your apartment.” He paused to listen to the other end of the phone. “Mom, no is not an answer here. You are in big trouble and you’re going to talk to us whether you want to or not.” Andrew raised his voice. “I don’t care, this is how it’s gonna be. What time do you get off work?” Another pause. “We’ll be there at 4:30.”

“I take it your mother did not want us to come?” I asked to verify what I knew was the answer to the question.

“You’ve got it. She said she would handle it herself. She would have been yelling if she wasn’t sitting at the receptionist desk where she works. Glad I called her there.”

“I’m sure she doesn’t want the probation officer to know, and she sure doesn’t want us coming. Let me call your father and break the news to him.”

I called Jim and told him the sordid story. He didn’t sound shocked. I guess by now nothing would surprise him about his ex-wife and my sister.

When I got off Andrew’s office phone, Andrew was quick to ask, “Well, what did Dad say?”

“He’s calling the probation officer now to let him know he better set up a meeting with Andrea and he told him we are going over to Andrea’s apartment late today.

He said he'll meet us here at two since it is another two hours to get there, we'll go together."

Andrea had her efficiency apartment in the same town as the prison where Greg was. I couldn't help but wonder whether Greg knew what Andrea had gotten herself into.

Andrew and I worked the rest of the day reviewing what additional information we had for our expose on the status of nursing homes. Through all of this, we couldn't help but wonder whether Greg's parents, who were nursing homeowners, had been supporting Greg in his endeavors to increase enrollment in the three large facilities they owned. That had not been proven in the case that sent Greg to prison. Greg was found guilty of delivering prescriptions to the wrong people, like he had done to my father. Greg never implicated his parents, but we knew they had to be guilty. We just hadn't proven it yet.

We were ready for a break, albeit not a pleasant one, when Jim came to pick us up to make the trip to Andrea's apartment. On the drive, we rehashed how Andrea could have gotten herself in such a mess and agreed that if someone had offered her a modeling job, she would be in her glory, and frankly she was just dumb enough to be gullible to this scam.

From the back seat, Andrew said, "What's the probation officer going to do with this information? How is he going to protect my mother?" Even though Andrew had gone through very trying times with his mother, I knew from many talks with him and when I looked into his eyes right at that moment, that he loved her and was protective of her. Andrea was his mother.

From the driver's seat, Jim turned down the radio and said, "He's shocked by this development and said he was going to call your mother and tell her he had to see her tomorrow. Maybe he can do something to get the threats to stop." Jim stopped to look so he could merge into the next lane and continued. "Andrew, I told him I'm concerned about you. This cat, Marcus, threatened you."

"I'll be okay, Dad, but how is Mother going to get out of this?"

His dad answered, "I wish I knew, son, I wish I knew."

Andrea's apartment was in a nice enough building, but it was a small efficiency. It was immaculate, as we expected. Andrea probably spent every waking moment cleaning the little space. The reality and sadness of her situation overcame me. My sister had always treated me horrible, but never did I want her life to be like this. There were only two kitchen chairs and a sofa bed, so Jim and I sat on the sofa bed and Andrea and her son sat on the two chairs.

Jim began the conversation, "Andrea, you need to level with us. What have you gotten yourself into? Who is this Marcus and what kind of modeling have you done for him?"

Andrea spoke in a soft tone, like she was afraid her little apartment was bugged "I was introduced to Marcus at the club several years ago. He was having lunch with someone there. He followed me, when I left, to the parking lot and introduced himself and told me how he was stricken by my beauty and that he was an agent for models. He asked me to meet him for dinner that night. I called Greg and told him I had a meeting and wouldn't see him that evening until later." She started sniffling, "He said he would get me modeling jobs."

"Let me guess, he asked you to pay him a fee?" Jim asked while he squeezed his eyes shut.

"That's right." Andrea shook her head.

"Just how much were you paying him a month, Andrea?" I knew where this was going. That's why she couldn't pay the "rent" to Greg's parents.

"Well, it really isn't any of your business, sister." Andrea frowned at me.

"Oh, but it is, Andrea, tell us now how much you were paying this scumbag?" Jim raised his voice since she had to be using the alimony Jim was giving her to pay this Marcus.

"Just $1500 a month, that's all." Andrea answered almost in a whisper. "And I did get some photo shoots."

Jim was losing his patience. "I gave you $2000 a month, where did the other $500 go."

"My shoots with the photographer required a different wardrobe every time." Andrea answered.

I spoke up, asking a question that I dreaded having her answer. "What kind of modeling was this, Andrea? what kind of clothes were you wearing?" I paused, "And in some of those photo shoots were you ever without clothes?"

Andrea stood up, "How dare you ask me that! what kind of woman do you think I am? I never posed with no clothes. I was a lingerie model. I was going to appear in catalogues for a very prestigious store."

"Were you ever in those catalogues, Mom?" Andrew asked.

"Marcus was working on it and felt I was about to have my big break anytime."

"Mom, I checked this Marcus out. He does porn films." I could see Andrew's throat as he swallowed hard and asked, "Mom, have you been in one of those films."

Andrea broke down and cried and sat back down. "Yes."

Andrew stood up and yelled, "How could you do something like that? Are you that stupid?"

Jim stood up and put his arm around Andrew, "Andrea, your son asked you how you did something so awful, and we want to hear the answer." Jim got loud, "Now."

I now had gotten up and was pacing the small little apartment, which felt like a cage at this point.

Andrea was sniffling. "He told me one afternoon that I was so beautiful, and he was in love with me. He took me to his apartment and one thing led to another." By this time, Andrea was weeping. "He tricked me. He must have had a camera on."

Jim put his hand to his head, "You think, Andrea? Weren't you a little suspicious?"

She continued, "A couple of days later, he showed me the film he made and told me he was going to share it. If I didn't keep paying him, he was going to tell Greg and his parents. What could I do? He laughed and said, 'you wanted to be a model, you got what you wanted'."

Chapter Sixty-eight

Fall, 1994

I was gazing out the window of my office at the university as I prepared for my last class before the Thanksgiving holiday would begin. The beautiful leaves that had decorated my view just one month earlier were gone, a reminder that the chill of winter was approaching.

I felt a brief sense of the cold air on me as I thought about my sister. I was looking forward to the holidays with Jim, Andrew, Mama, and Papa. We didn't know whether Andrea would join us or not. We had invited her for Thanksgiving, but she claimed to have plans.

My anger for the way she had treated me for so many years had been replaced with pity. Andrea had a serious mental illness that prevented her from living a normal life. Her need for perfection could have been channeled in a positive direction, but in her zeal to be a star, she had created an untenable situation for herself. In her quest to be better than everyone else, she had demeaned and hurt so many others along the way. Her life had taken the wrong fork in the road.

When we learned that she had been in a porn flick, we had told the probation officer after that awkward visit we had with her in the tiny little apartment where she now lived. While it was neat and clean, it didn't meet with her expectations for what she had wanted her life to be, and what it had been while she was living with Greg and being supported by her ex-husband.

The officer had discovered that this modeling agent, Marcus, was involved in was quite a pornographic ring and with some good investigation he was arrested and was awaiting trial for trafficking of young girls. We had found it interesting that he was interested in Andrea.

My phone rang, startling me out of my daydreaming. I heard from the other end of the phone, "Hey Tice, when are you coming home?"

"One more class in thirty minutes for an hour, and then I'm on the way." I looked at my watch to see what the time was. "How's it going?"

I heard Andrew give me some good news. "I got the final edits on our book today. They look good so maybe we can spend time over the holidays dealing with some last-minute issues."

Our book about the nursing home industry was almost a reality. Andrew continued, "The real reason I'm calling though is to let you know about Marcus."

I braced myself for some bad news because Marcus was a slimy character and his trial had been taking place over the last two weeks. "Don't tell me he got off."

"He sure didn't, but it's complicated and I don't want to give you all the details over the phone so get home as soon as you can. I'll be waiting for you. I think Dad said he is making us a light dinner because we'll stuff ourselves at Grandma and Grandpa's tomorrow."

I laughed, "Well, you've got me curious, and I'll call you after class to let you know I'm on the way."

What a relief it was to hear that Marcus didn't get off for all the horrible things he had done, but what else was going on?

I was soon to find out. I had the best husband in the world who had a bottle of Moscato chilling, the table set, and dinner ready when I arrived home. We had not moved into our new home yet. It was to be ready by spring. "What's this? I think I hit the jackpot for the best husband ever."

Jim answered, "I understand a celebration is in order. Your new book with Andrew is one step closer to reality."

I hugged Jim and looked at my nephew, "I guess you've already shared the news."

"Sure did, but I haven't told either of you the most interesting news of the day. Let's sit down and I'll tell you over dinner." Andrew pulled the chair out for me.

"Wait a minute. I thought this was going to be a light meal because we're going to be pigging out tomorrow." I patted my stomach.

"Oh, it's just some lasagna I made and a salad." Jim started tossing the salad and putting it in our salad bowls.

"Looks yummy, Dad. Let me pour the wine. We've got Moscato for Tice, but I brought some red wine also for the pasta. What do you want, Tice?"

"I'll try the red and we can save the Moscato for later." I had a happy thought about taking my glass of wine into the bedroom after dinner when Jim and I were alone.

As we ate our lasagna and oohed about how wonderful it was, Andrew disclosed the story of the day. "I got a call this afternoon from one of my sources."

"About what?" Jim took a drink of his wine and leaned forward. "Didn't you say Marcus is going to serve time? That scumbag deserves it. And then we find out he was engaged in sex trafficking. I hope they put him away for a long time."

Andrew swallowed his bite of lasagna. "Well, he won't get as many years as he might have."

I was confused, "What do you mean?"

"It seems he is talking and, according to my source, he's talking about Greg's parents."

Andrew stopped as I asked. "What do you mean, what's going on?"

Jim refilled our glasses of wine. Andrew continued. "This is all coming out in the paper tomorrow. Greg's parents were part of the porn business that Marcus was running."

"I thought they were in the nursing home business." Jim had put his wine down on this news.

"That's right but they're also in the porn business and were funding Marcus, but here's the kicker," Andrew quit eating. "They were giving names of gullible women to Marcus so he could lure them into his modeling business."

"Oh no." I said as my eyes got big, and my mouth got very dry.

"Yes, they set my mother up and once she made the film, they threatened her and told her they would tell Greg if she said anything." There were tiny tears in his eyes as he said, "Greg's parents paid this guy to set my mother up to be in a porn film and then blackmailed her."

Chapter Sixty-nine

Fall, 1994

Jim, Andrew, and I collapsed on the couch late Thanksgiving afternoon. We had such a delightful time cooking dinner as a team. Mama had supervised the big event, but we had done much of the cooking, while Papa arranged the table and marveled at the production of this meal. Mama was still in the kitchen making sure everything was cleaned up to her satisfaction.

The food from the turkey to the mashed potatoes to the pumpkin and mincemeat pies had been excellent, if I did say so myself. Mama's stroke had slowed her down and, coupled with the heartbreak of Andrea's ordeal, her health and emotional strength was declining. Her obsessive-compulsive behaviors had become worse. We just let her keep cleaning the kitchen. It was hard to watch, but we tried to keep things upbeat and positive.

Mama was looking at her watch as she came out of the kitchen and sat down in her usual chair in the living room. "It's four o'clock. Why hasn't Andrea called? She always calls us today. It's tradition."

I looked at Andrew and his brows were furrowed with worry. I knew he had snuck away several times to call his mother and there had been no answer.

"Mama, maybe she's still visiting her friend and doesn't have access to a telephone." My statement was true. She had told us she was going to visit Greg at the prison, and she may not have gotten to the phone. I hoped this was her reason and not her selfishness showing through. I had watched my sister snap my mother's heart. I had also watched Mama's slow realization that her daughter was not who she thought she was. Mama had witnessed how Andrea had decreased her contact with her since her stroke. Only when Andrea needed something, like wanting to move in when she had no other place to go, did my sister contact Mama.

"Well, I wish she would have come for Thanksgiving. She would have been a big help to me." Mama said with a sigh.

Jim changed the subject. "Annie, that meal was superb, and nobody bakes a mincemeat pie like you do. I need to get the recipe so I can make it for Tice because she loves it."

Mama beamed as she answered, "Thanks, Jim, let me go out to the kitchen right now and I'll write it down for you."

As she left us, Andrew whispered, "I have been calling my mom's apartment and no answer. You'd think she would be back from the prison by now."

In a low tone of voice, Jim answered, "Why don't you call the prison and see if they will tell you whether she was there." He paused. "I know Andrea didn't want to come here, but you would think she would call her own mother."

"Good idea, Dad. I'll put on my investigative hat and call and see what I can find out." "I just have this nagging feeling that something's wrong."

"I'm with you, Andrew, something isn't quite right, and I just can't put my finger on it." I had a knot in the pit of my stomach that my sister was doing something but what was it?

Papa had been dozing and woke up, still in a sleep awakening fog. "Has Andrea called?"

"No, Grandpa, and I'm going to go make some phone calls." Andrew headed to what had been my bedroom where there was an extension phone. "Keep Grandma busy so she doesn't pick up the phone. I don't want her to know I'm calling a prison." We had not told Mama that Andrea's boyfriend was in prison, but she may have known from the newspaper. She didn't seem to pay much attention to the news since her stroke, but the word prison would be disturbing to her.

Jim and Papa watched the football game which, by their own waning interest, seemed to be a bit boring. I leafed through the Thanksgiving newspaper, planning for our black Friday excursions, an activity I loved to do, and Jim tolerated to keep me happy.

Andrew came out of the bedroom, he frowned and in a low voice said, “This is strange. The prison warden on duty said she never showed up and Greg has been very agitated because she was supposed to be there at eleven this morning.”

“That is strange. Why would she tell him she was coming and then not show up?” I asked.

“I’m afraid there’s more to the story.” Andrew paused with a look of fear. “Since he didn’t have his visitor and, very interesting, his parents never came to visit and didn’t call, they let me talk to Greg.”

“I’m surprised at that,” Jim got up and turned the TV down.

“Well, I guess they think they should be nice on Thanksgiving.” Andrew answered.

“So, what did Greg say to you?” I put the newspaper down.

“He said she called at ten this morning. She was almost incoherent, but she slurred her words as she said something like why you did what you did to me, I always loved you.”

Jim stood up and looked at me and Andrew, “Get your coats, we have to get to Andrea’s apartment.”

Chapter Seventy

Fall, 1994

On Thanksgiving night, the roads were clear of the usual everyday traffic. Families and friends were snuggled at home, bemoaning the fact that they had eaten too much turkey, dressing, and pie. We had that same feeling but also a sinking fear that something was wrong with Andrea. Where was she?

"What do you make of all this?" Jim asked Andrew and me. "Have I overreacted having us jump in the car to check out what's going on?"

"No, Dad, something is very wrong. Why didn't mom answer her phone all day? Why did she call Greg and ask why he had done something to her? Granted he was a sleaze bag, as was his whole family, but Greg didn't know anything about what Andrea had done with her modeling agent."

"I have a knot in the pit of my stomach and the beginning of a headache that something's going on." I said as I rubbed my head. "Here is another question I have."

"What's that?" Jim asked as he put his hand on my forehead when we stopped at a traffic light.

"Why didn't Greg's parents come to see him today in prison? After all, it is Thanksgiving?" I answered.

"I am wondering the same thing," Andrew said as he sat up from the back seat and leaned forward. "You would think they would have come to see their only son on a holiday." He sighed as he added, "Then again, this is the first Thanksgiving, my mom didn't come to see me. With all her flaws, she always saw me on Thanksgiving and Christmas."

Jim looked back at Andrew, "Well, maybe there's a good reason for what she's done. Let's just hope for the best."

I looked down at my feet, "Oh my gosh, in our rush to get out the door, I still have on my house slippers. Andrea will really let me have it for going out in public with these on. I can just hear her now." I laughed as I was trying to ease the tension that Andrew must be having about his mother. "You never go out in public with bathroom slippers on."

"Oh, Tice, mother is always so concerned about her perfect image that she just cannot understand why you don't put fashion first." Andrew paused. "If only she could see that there is so much more to life than cleaning and fashion."

Jim looked back at his son and with a resigned look on his face responded, "I know, Andrew, but your mother is who she is, and we can't change her. You know,

I'm wondering whether she may have gotten drunk so she wouldn't have to face this day alone."

"You may be right, Jim, she has to be lonely." I was just hoping that we would find her okay and with some plausible explanation for why she hadn't contacted her son. In the back of my mind, I was wondering whether something else had happened, maybe with Greg's parents. I put that ugly thought out of my head, "Do you think we should have alerted her probation officer?"

"I think, even though it's Thanksgiving, when we get there, I'll give him a call," Jim answered.

"Who's got the key to Andrea's apartment? How will we get in?" I asked.

Andrew reached into his pocket and showed the key. "Dad gave me a key in case I ever needed it. Glad you did, since mom might not let us in."

Jim laughed, "I brought my key too, since I'm paying her rent directly to the landlord, I have one and gave you one, son." Jim had arranged with the probation officer that he would be responsible for the lease on the apartment. Her pay for her job as a receptionist was not much. He had been afraid Andrea would give any money that Jim gave her to Marcus or Greg's parents. She was being blackmailed by all of them.

We pulled into the parking lot of the apartment building. Andrea's car was in the lot. "Well, she's here unless she went out with someone."

"Look Dad and Tice, mother's lights are not on in her apartment." Andrew commented as he pointed up to her window.

"Maybe, she's sleeping the day off," Jim commented as he turned off the motor. I hoped that Jim was right.

We took the elevator up to her fourth-floor apartment and walked down the hall. Andrew knocked on the door. There was no answer. He knocked again. Still no answer. Jim yelled out, "Andrea, are you in there? Let us in or we're coming in."

The neighbor across the hall came out, "Hey what's all the racket? I'm tired. Can you keep it down?"

"Sorry about that," Andrew answered, "Have you seen my mom today?"

"Just saw her when she let her company in. I wouldn't ordinarily pay any attention, but I was taking my garbage out."

"Oh, who was her company?" I asked. "I'm her sister and we are wondering about her and what she did for Thanksgiving?"

"Well, I don't think they were there very long because I heard the door slam just a little while later."

"Do you remember who they were?" Jim asked.

"They were an older couple, well dressed and very snooty. Don't even speak to me when I see them in the hall."

"Do they come to see her very often?" Andrew asked.

"Look, I'm not nosey and it's none of my business what the lady does, but they're here, maybe once a week. I gotta go. My hubby wants his supper. Leftovers you know from our big turkey dinner."

Andrew turned the key in the lock and opened the door to a dark room that smelled of Andrea's favorite perfume, Youth Dew. Jim found the light and turned it on. There on her bed was his ex-wife. She was sleeping. She must have dozed off with her clothes on. She had one of her nice dresses on, pearls around her neck, and even earrings.

Andrew shook her to wake her up, "Mom, mom, wake up." He rolled her over. He gasped. "Dad, Tice, she's not breathing. I think she's," he started sobbing, "I think she's dead."

Chapter Seventy-one

Fall, 2000

It had been six years since that fateful day when Andrew had found his mother dead from an overdose. Every Thanksgiving reminded me of that time, and I knew that this holiday was the hardest for my nephew, so we always had a quiet dinner at our home.

The autopsy showed what we feared that Andrea had committed suicide, but for the next year we had doubts about whether Greg's parents had drugged her. After an investigation, we learned that Greg's parents had visited Andrea, just like the nosy neighbor had said. They had visited often, apparently threatening Andrea if she didn't give them money, but they denied that they had anything to do with her death. Their prints were never found on the pill bottle. There was not a suicide note but Andrea must have planned it and even as she was killing herself, she had to be dressed up in one of her beautiful dresses and her pearls.

I heard the doorbell and yelled in the kitchen at Jim, "I'll get it." Andrew was there carrying my beautiful little great niece, Annie. "Oh, look at you and your pretty little dress. Where did you get that?" Andrew put her in my arms. I felt so much love for this child. Annie pointed to her mother, Teresa. Teresa had provided a great deal of comfort to my nephew when he was grieving over the death of his mother, and they got married three months after that. Annie pointed to her mother, "Mommy got it; it was a surprise." Annie had been named after my mother. Andrew had always loved spending time with his grandma and grandpa.

"Well, let's go show this surprise to Grandpa Jim and Paw Paw." Mama had died six months after Andrea's death. She had given up with the news that her adored and perfect daughter had died, and we watched her health deteriorate. We had never told Mama the circumstances of Andrea's death. We just told her we found her dead and her heart must have given out.

Andrew turned to his wife and said, "Teresa kind of got carried away and has several dishes she baked in the car. I'll go get them while you show off Annie's dress to everyone."

"Teresa, you put me to shame as a cook. What did you make for today? I told you it wasn't necessary," I paused, "but I sure hope you brought your cranberry relish and pineapple casserole."

"I sure did, Aunt Tice, and a new recipe I tried for Brussel sprouts." Teresa kissed me on the cheek. I was so happy that Andrew had met this wonderful young lady who was a third-grade teacher. I loved to hear her talk about her students, it brought back memories of the teachers who had helped me along the way, especially the one who encouraged me to write the essay about Papa that won the state contest. Teresa continued, "only the best for you."

"Hey, where's my little Annie?" Jim came out of the kitchen with his apron and chef hat on. Annie giggled, "Grandpa, you look silly. Look at my new dress."

"Oh, look at that little turkey on your dress." Jim said as he reached to take Annie from me. He gave a peck on the cheek to Teresa. "What's this, you came empty handed?"

"Not quite, Jim, she made several dishes and even brought a new recipe." I answered.

Jim put Annie down, "Go see Paw Paw and show him your dress."

Annie ran over to Paw Paw who was sitting in his recliner. "Look at my new dress." Papa picked Annie up and put him on her lap. Annie straightened out her little dress right away and picked a little speck that was on it right away.

"What's wrong," Papa said? Annie looked down at her dress," Paw Paw, my dress has a spot on it."

"Oh no, where is it?" Papa asked.

"Right here." Annie pointed to a tiny spot.

Paw Paw looked at the small piece of dirt on her dress. "Look Annie, it's magic, I made it go away." Annie hugged my father. That small gesture brought back all the times that Papa had made the hurt I felt from either Mama or my sister go away.

Papa had come to live with us when we got our new home built. We had built a special wing of the house so that Mama and Papa both could live with us some day. Mama died before that could happen. Papa wasn't sure he wanted to leave his home but realized he was lonely, and it was tough for him to cook and clean on his own. I loved watching the joy that little Annie brought him and all of us. She was a loving child. I hoped that Teresa and Andrew would have more children, now that they were both settled in their positions. Andrew had gotten the job as editor of the paper where I had been in the same position. We had finished the book some time ago on the nursing home scandals and had won several awards for it. I was remembering so much today trying to focus on what was positive in our lives, but Andrea's death lurked in the back of my mind. It seemed like I always lived in her shadow even after her death.

Paw Paw read Annie's favorite story to her, *The Little Engine that Could.* When he left out a word, Annie was quick to point it out to him and he had read it through three times before Jim called his famous, "Dinner is served." announcement.

"Dear, you are the greatest cook." I said as I took a whiff of the dressing that Jim had made. "And Teresa, you are top notch yourself. I can't wait to dig into the Brussel sprouts." I looked at the green casserole with buttered bread crumbs on top of it.

"Well, the table is absolutely beautiful and I know Aunt Tice did that." Teresa said as she rubbed her hand across the tablecloth.

"Can I sit next to Aunt Tice?" Annie pointed to me.

"You sure can, young lady, but I thought you wanted to sit next to me." Jim made a face like he was pouting.

"I'll sit next to you too, Grandpa, and Aunt Tice can be on the other side." Jim got her booster seat from the kitchen and lifted her into the chair. "There you go, young lady." Teresa put a bib around Annie's neck.

As we all sat down to a wonderful looking meal and Andrew poured the fizzling champagne for each of us, Jim said, "I want to propose a toast to all of you at this table. May we be blessed for many years to come with as much happiness as we have today."

We all clicked our glasses and said, "Hear, hear." I added, "And to the chefs for today."

Jim stood up to carve the golden-brown turkey as we began passing the dishes around. Teresa spooned some mashed potatoes onto Annie's plate. She was careful to put the green beans away from the mashed potatoes and put the cranberry salad on a separate plate for her. Jim went to serve her turkey and as he started to put it on her plate, she cried, "No Grandpa, I have to have another plate for my turkey."